FANTA

Cold Blood 1

FINAL ACT

Robin Campbell

Cold Blood 1

FINAL ACT

FANTAIL

FANTAIL BOOKS

Published by the Penguin Group
Penguin Books Ltd, 27 Wrights Lane, London W8 5TZ, England
Penguin Books USA Inc., 375 Hudson Street, New York, New York 10014, USA
Penguin Books Australia Ltd, Ringwood, Victoria, Australia
Penguin Books Canada Ltd, 10 Alcorn Avenue, Toronto, Ontario, Canada M4V 3B2
Penguin Books (NZ) Ltd, 182–190 Wairau Road, Auckland 10, New Zealand

Penguin Books Ltd, Registered Offices: Harmondsworth, Middlesex, England

First published 1994
1 3 5 7 9 10 8 6 4 2

The moral right of the author has been asserted

Typeset by Datix International Limited, Bungay, Suffolk
Printed in England by Clays Ltd, St Ives plc
Filmset in Monophoto Palatino

One

I'M WATCHING YOU – YOU CAN'T
ESCAPE ME

The garishly coloured letters, carelessly chopped out of magazines and glued haphazardly on to plain paper, gave the note a comic look, but the message was icily clear and sent a shiver down Sophie's spine. She was instantly aware of the dreaded sensation of cold tendrils stealthily threading around her, determined to drag her back to her old way of life; the life which Sophie had struggled so hard to escape.

Though the note was naturally anonymous, Sophie had no doubt about who'd sent it. It could only have been the product of Carl's cruel mind. Any normal person would have written a real letter, made a phone call, or simply stopped her in the street. Only Carl had the twisted tenacity needed to pursue her halfway across the country and then, having succeeded in finding her, the desire to stand back and take sadistic pleasure from watching her squirm, before he eventually pounced.

1

But Carl's power over her was so strong, Sophie only had to read his words to feel everything she'd hoped to achieve by running away from him to start a new life beginning to ebb away. Sophie could feel herself regressing into her old self, compliant as a rag doll. From bitter experience, she knew putting up a fight would be useless. Even if he didn't resort to violence, on the rare occasions she'd offered the slightest resistance to any of his self-centred suggestions, he'd taken enormous pleasure in wearing her down, the relentless way dripping water finally erodes stone. She had no choice but to give in to Carl, just as she always had.

'Something wrong, Sophie?'

Sophie's mind had travelled so far back, when she turned she was amazed to find herself still in front of the post-rack on the dimly-lit landing. The tall figure of Oliver stood just inside the stage door. The evening mist had frosted his dark, unruly hair so that it twinkled slightly under the naked bulb, giving an almost halo-like effect. His patient, velvet-brown eyes looked genuinely concerned.

'No,' she said quickly, stuffing the note in her pocket and trying to ignore the cold hand of fear clutching at her stomach, 'it's nothing. Nothing at all.'

'If you say so,' Oliver agreed pleasantly, 'but when I came through that door I could have sworn you'd just seen a ghost.'

More a spectre than a ghost, Sophie thought grimly, but she forced a smile. 'Come on, we're late for rehearsal as it is.' Sophie led the way through the swing-doors.

*

The auditorium was wheel shaped; the acting area its hub. From it, six aisles ran out like spokes and between them were curved, rising tiers of seats for the audience. The whole thing looked a little like a rather sombre circus, with the stage as the ring.

Sophie had always thought of theatres as being bright and lively, but during rehearsals it was very different. The cast, currently sitting in the acting area, were lit only from above by a single working-light, which cast cold shadows, blanking out the actors' eyes, leaving dark, hollow sockets. But there was still the rich, familiar smell.

The theatre had been converted from the lower floors of an old mill and the huge, rough-hewn, oak beams, which formed the building's main frame, were heavily impregnated with a thick treacly smell, resulting from over a century of grinding grain into flour.

Since then, the Mill had had a curiously chequered history. Following fifty years of neglect and vandalism, a society had been formed to restore it, but they'd been forced to contend not only with the derelict machinery, but also the fabric of the building, replacing crumbling bricks and mortar, rotting window frames, broken glass, worm-eaten planks and missing slates. Sadly, by the time the bulk of the work was done, the society ran out of funds and were forced to let part of it, leaving Eddie, as caretaker-cum-odd job man, to guard their interests.

A small professional theatre company, liking the secluded riverside setting, rented two floors, but, strangely, having gone to all the trouble and expense of converting the ground floor and basement into a fully-equipped theatre, complete with a foyer and dressing-rooms, they had mysteriously disappeared without trace. Rumours of bad debts were immediately disproved and there appeared to be no logical explanation. Again the gaunt building stood empty, until Nathan formed an amateur company and moved in.

'After all, can you think of a better setting,' Nathan had asked, 'for a story about cruelty and witchcraft?'

From the first moment she walked in, Sophie certainly believed there was something eerie about the place. It wasn't merely the sound of rats scuttling hungrily across the bare boards of the floor above their heads, or even the rooks which circled the place by day, having invaded the roof space for their nests. Nor was it the dark, narrow, cobwebbed corridors which honeycombed the building, opening on to all kinds of odd rooms, some no more than dusty nooks and crannies. What made Sophie's heart jump most was the startling way the oak timbers unexpectedly cracked and snapped as they suddenly responded to changes of temperature and humidity. That constant shifting always gave her the weird feeling she was not inside a building, more a huge, living, breathing animal.

Sophie slipped into an empty seat beside Paula, a bubbly redhead, who raised a quizzical eyebrow above her gorgeous sea-green eyes as she whispered, 'And what have you two been up to?'

'Nothing whatever,' Sophie insisted. 'We just happened to arrive together, that's all.'

'I'll believe you.' Paula grinned. She was determined to make them an item, but so far, though not because of any lack of interest on Oliver's part, more from

Sophie's unspoken determination not to get involved with another guy so soon after escaping from Carl, she had failed.

However, that was Paula's only failure. From the moment Sophie had arrived in town four months previously, Paula, whom Sophie had accidentally bumped into in a boutique, trying to decide how much freckled flesh to bare at the disco, had taken full control of Sophie's life. Not only had Paula got her a job in the office where she worked, but she'd found her a delightful little flat opposite the park and then, to crown it all, and take care of Sophie's social life while she settled down in a strange town, she'd persuaded her to join the amateur dramatic group.

'It's terrific fun,' Paula enthused. 'We're making all our own costumes and everything!'

'Hang on a minute,' Sophie had protested. 'I've never acted in my entire life! I even hate having to read aloud.'

'That won't be a problem,' Paula assured her. 'We haven't got a script yet.'

Sophie was horrified. 'You mean we have to make the words up as we go along?'

'Not exactly. It's a group project.'

The Testing of Agnes Wishart was to be based on a local seventeenth-century legend about an exceptionally beautiful young girl accused of being a witch. When she refused to confess her sins, even under brutal torture at the hands of the infamous witch-hunter, Mathew Hopkins, she was condemned to be burnt at the stake. By the time Agnes's original accuser, a spurned suitor, was driven mad by guilt and confessed on his deathbed, Agnes had already died a horrible death – though her ghost was still believed to haunt evildoers in the town.

Amongst the cast of twelve some, like Oliver, played one part, while others had several smaller roles and also appeared in the chorus, sometimes dressed as villagers, but towards the end they wore black robes and skull masks as evil spirits. Pete, in a grey robe, was the Narrator, who linked the scenes of the play, talking directly to the audience.

'We're doing all our own research,' Paula explained, 'then we bring our ideas to rehearsals and improvise around them until we're completely satisfied and before the script is written.'

Sophie's self-confidence had suffered badly while she'd been with Carl and, besides, she'd always hated making a fool of herself in public. She made one last desperate bid for freedom. 'I'm sure I'd be useless. I've never done anything like it.'

'Nor me,' Paula admitted happily, 'not until I joined the group. But they're a great crowd, you'll love them. Besides, the director, Nathan, was in the professional theatre until he became a teacher and he's very good at helping people, so you don't have to worry about a thing.'

Sophie had quickly discovered that attempting to resist the full force of Paula's enthusiasms was like trying to remain upright in a tidal wave.

Sophie had grown up so used to not being allowed to think for herself that it seemed the most natural thing in the world to allow Paula to sort everything out so competently. Sophie felt she'd only ever taken one *real* decision in her entire life, to leave Carl, and since the unexpected arrival of the note, even that isolated success was being called into question.

'Are you with us, Sophie?'

Sophie swam up through the oily green sea of her confused thoughts and realized she hadn't heard a word Nathan had been saying to her. 'I'm sorry . . .' she stammered apologetically.

From the moment she'd joined the group, Nathan had insisted she must play Agnes. Sophie's protests, as usual, were useless.

Nathan had thrust a colour photograph, taken from a contemporary miniature of Agnes Wishart, under her nose. 'Can't you see the likeness? You both have the same delicately-boned, heart-shaped faces; even your blue eyes and your straight, shoulder-length, blonde hair, are exactly the same shades. You've even got the same, almost translucent, milk-white skin.'

Sophie was forced to admit there was a similarity, though she didn't find the comparison to a witch, especially one who was burned to death, exactly comforting.

'But there's far more to it than that,' Nathan went on, narrowing his eyes as he peered thoughtfully through his glasses at Sophie. 'It's a particular quality about you . . .' Whilst Nathan struggled for the right word, his fingers absentmindedly searched through his hair, as if he might find it lurking amongst the tight curls. 'Vulnerability!' he cried triumphantly, and impaled the word, as it hung in the air, by stabbing it with a finger.

Oh yes, she thought bitterly. I'm vulnerable all right!

'Which is exactly what we need for Agnes.'

'Isn't someone already playing that part?' Sophie asked.

A tall thin girl with a prominent nose and short brown hair held up her hand. 'Yes, me. I'm Marge.'

'As you can see,' Nathan said, waving a hand towards Marge as if she were an exhibit, 'she isn't nearly as like Agnes as you are. For a start she'd need a wig.'

'I really don't want to push somebody else out of the leading role.'

Marge smiled. 'I honestly don't mind. I'd be far happier in the chorus and playing some minor part.'

'But it's the most important part in the play,' Sophie had insisted. 'Shouldn't you have an experienced actress for it?'

'Not really,' Nathan said with a curt shake of his head. 'Although Agnes is central to the entire production, how she looks is the absolutely crucial part. Despite being on stage almost all the time, you wouldn't be expected to do much apart from stand around looking beautiful but frail and pathetic.'

Typecast! Sophie thought grimly.

'Besides,' Paula added, 'from the day she was accused, Agnes refused to speak to anyone. So apart from moaning and screaming a lot while she's being tortured, it's really almost a non-speaking part and you won't have many lines to learn.'

That had clinched it. That and Oliver. When they'd first arrived, Sophie had been so embarrassed, having so many pairs of eyes staring in her direction, that she'd avoided looking at the rest of the cast. Then, slowly, uncoiling from what at first glance looked more like a shambolic pile of old clothes, emerged Oliver. It was as if somebody had thrown back an old, stained tarpaulin to reveal a gleaming Ferrari.

Not that Oliver's clothes hadn't once been good, but the colours seemed to have been washed out of his shirts, which were also frayed at the collars and cuffs, as were his faded, crumpled sweaters. His jeans were always bagged at the knee and loose threads from the hems trailed over scuffed trainers.

However, anything Oliver lacked in clothes-sense was more than made up for by his craggy good looks. Though probably only a little older than Sophie herself, his face had an experienced, lived-in look. On anyone else the faint scar, which straggled like a thin purple worm from his right eyebrow to disappear in the hair above his ear, might have been considered slightly disfiguring. But on Oliver's broad, open features, it only emphasized the perfection of the rest: his strong jaw, dreamy eyes, full, always half-smiling lips and perfect white teeth. Yet it was the scar, that and his dominating height, which made him ideal casting for the part of Mathew Hopkins, the cruel witch-hunter.

Nathan, with a sharp prod of his forefinger, impatiently thrust the shiny, metal-framed spectacles back up on to the bridge of his nose. 'I was asking if you have any suggestions as to how we might tackle the courtroom scene with the witch-hunter?'

Sophie hastily shook her head. Because everyone else was always coming up with such original ideas, during the day Sophie had given the scene a great deal of thought. But the arrival of that awful note had driven everything else from her mind. She walked through the remainder of the rehearsal like a zombie. During the torture scene, while the thumbscrews were applied, Nathan complained bitterly that Sophie's screams were not nearly sufficiently bloodcurdling. But that evening, try as she might, Sophie could produce little more than a whimper.

At the end of rehearsal, instead of hanging round to chat, she slipped quietly away, the first to leave. She paused on the steps outside the stage door to allow her eyes to grow accustomed to the darkness of the carpark. She peered through a thin veil of mist, cautiously searching amongst the parked cars and the banks of damp rhododendron bushes for the slightest sign of Carl. How long had he been silently watching her movements? Days, weeks perhaps?

Seeing nothing, Sophie walked quickly, anxiously counting the moments before she would reach the comparatively well-lit road. But she was only crossing the broad, stone river bridge, still in the shadow of the mill, when a heavy hand suddenly fell on her shoulder and she let out a piercing scream which echoed off the tall building.

Two

'That scream was more the sort of thing Nathan had in mind,' Oliver said with admiration.

But Sophie was in no mood for jokes. 'You frightened me to death.'

'I'm sorry, Sophie, you aren't normally so jumpy. Let me buy you a cup of coffee to make up for scaring you.'

Sophie knew she needed something to steady her nerves but, if Carl really was following her, was it a good idea to be seen with Oliver? But then Carl's note suggested he'd been watching her movements for some time, so he must already have known that after rehearsals Sophie often stopped off somewhere. Sometimes with the others, but often alone with Oliver. Besides, Carl was so unpredictable and, not knowing exactly when he would make his next move, or precisely what form that would take, she found Oliver's bulky presence comforting.

'OK, yes please.' Sophie shucked up the collar of her navy blue reefer jacket to keep out the cold mist which swirled around them.

As the long-legged Oliver strode off towards town and Sophie hurried to keep up, the headlights of cars belonging to other members of the cast, swept over them.

'Why don't you have a car, Oliver?'

'Because I don't drive.'

Sophie found that slightly odd. Although Oliver dressed like a fugitive from Oxfam, she knew he had an extremely good job, as an artist with a successful advertising agency, and could hardly be short of money.

'Besides,' he went on, 'why waste the world's energy resources when I've got two perfectly good legs which can take me to most places I want to go?'

Oliver's concern for others was yet another aspect of his character which appealed to Sophie. It was such a refreshing change after Carl's self-centred attitude. Carl would have happily burned the world's last shovelful of coal for his own personal comfort.

The brisk walk in the night air did Sophie good, especially when they reached the well-lit streets of the town and there had been no sign of Carl. Oliver found a quiet table in the corner of the friendly Italian café and Sophie ordered a cappuccino, which their usual waiter, Dario, automatically sprinkled with extra chocolate.

'Are you beginning to settle down now?' Oliver asked.

'What do you mean?'

'New place to live, new job; they all take a while to adjust to.'

'Oh yes,' Sophie said, 'everyone's been so kind.'

'Is this the first time you've lived away from home?'

'Yes it is.' Sophie hated talking about her past. From the beginning she'd decided, if she was ever to succeed in off-loading the weight of emotional baggage she carried and make a fresh start, the less people knew about her past, the better. The only exception had been the glowing reference from her previous employer, but that was now safely locked away in the confidential personnel files.

'Odd, isn't it?' Oliver stirred his coffee. 'You never realize, until you move away from your parents, quite how much you've been depending on them.'

Sophie wanted to divert attention away from herself. 'Are your parents still alive?'

'Yes, though I haven't seen much of them for a while.'

Sophie was surprised by the shadow which passed over Oliver's face. 'Why, don't you get on?'

'Oh, yes, it's not that,' he replied, 'but they live a long way off and I don't seem to find the time to visit.'

Sophie couldn't help noticing that Oliver didn't say exactly where they lived. In many ways Oliver was no more forthcoming about his past than she was. Maybe he had something to hide too. But, of course, that was nonsense. Oliver was a perfectly nice guy who preferred living in the present. He'd said as much before, when he'd once mentioned his art college, though without naming it. Sophie had asked if he kept in touch with any of his mates from those days.

'Not really,' Oliver said. 'Once something's over, it's over. I've moved on, grown up and got new friends. You can't live life constantly looking over your shoulder. There's enough to cope with day by day, in the present.'

Ever since she'd arrived in town, that was certainly the philosophy of life Sophie had tried to adopt, though the arrival of Carl's note had suddenly changed all that.

'So,' Oliver broke across her thoughts, 'are you getting any happier about being in the play?'

'I suppose so, but I'm still not sure I enjoy being thought of as a witch,' Sophie said with a smile.

'Ah, but the whole point of the play is discovering you weren't a witch,' Oliver said. 'Though I have to say, you being Agnes is starting to make it difficult for me to be as evil as I should, playing Mathew Hopkins.'

Sophie was puzzled. 'Why?'

Oliver looked her straight in the eyes as he gently laid his warm, strong hand over hers and said, in a mock-romantic voice, 'Because you are so very bewitching.'

In spite of the jokey tone, Sophie felt herself blush. Oh, if only they hadn't met so soon after her escape from the traumatic relationship with Carl she might be more certain of her true feelings about Oliver. Maybe he only seemed so attractive because she was still busy running very hard from Carl?

Either way, although she was flattered by his attentions, thoroughly enjoyed his friendship and, above all, was grateful now for the protection he offered, Sophie knew she wasn't ready yet, to get involved in another serious relationship. Added to which, Sophie thought there was something decidedly odd about somebody as dishy as Oliver not already having a regular girlfriend, though that was the impression, confirmed by Paula, he'd always given.

Sophie gently withdrew her hand from under Oliver's. 'If you're worried about your acting,' she said, 'then I wouldn't have thought getting any friendlier with your intended victim would help your characterization.'

Oliver gave an exaggerated sigh as he reluctantly agreed. 'I suppose you're right. But can't I even tempt you to another coffee?' he asked, and then, putting on the evil leer he used so effectively as Mathew, added, 'Or perhaps something stronger?'

Sophie laughed. That was the great thing about Oliver – unlike Carl, he didn't take everything she said to heart and instantly do a moody. It was a long time since anyone had made her laugh. 'No thanks. I think I ought to be getting home.'

'Would you like me to walk you back?'

'Still determined to try and have your wicked way with me?' Sophie grinned.

'Well, I was hoping for another cup of coffee,' Oliver leered, 'but I'll settle for biting your neck and imbibing a few pints of your warm blood instead!'

In spite of the jokes, Sophie was relieved to have Oliver's company. Outside the café the swirling mist, which still hung in the street, had been reinforced by a biting wind. Several times during the short walk back to her flat, she was convinced she heard the sound of a footfall behind her. But every time she'd spun round, there was nothing more sinister to see than a stray cat or dog crossing the deserted street.

As they passed the entrance to a darkened alley, a white paper bag was suddenly tossed up towards Sophie's face by the gusty wind. Sophie jumped back in alarm.

Oliver put a comforting arm round her shoulder. 'Something *is* bothering you tonight.'

Sophie, realizing her hand had been unconsciously clutching Carl's note in her pocket, guiltily released it before she said, 'No, it's nothing. I'm just being silly, that's all.'

Again, shortly after they'd turned into Sophie's road, where the streetlights were fewer and less powerful, they were walking alongside the park railings, when Sophie was startled by a sharp scurrying clatter on the pavement behind her, like a clawed beast pursuing her. She cried out loud and buried her face in Oliver's chest.

Oliver folded his arms protectively around her. 'Sophie, it's only some old dead leaves being blown along by the wind. Look, if you tell me what's bothering you, maybe I could help?'

Sophie pulled away from him. 'I've already said, there's nothing!' she snapped, 'So leave it!'

Oliver shrugged. 'Suit yourself.'

Sophie knew it wasn't fair to take it out on poor Oliver, and when they reached the safety of a pool of light outside her gate, she turned to look up at him. 'Oliver, I'm sorry, I didn't mean to snap at you. It's been a long day and I'm a bit tired.'

Oliver took her hands in his and said gently, 'It's you I'm worried about, not me.'

'I'll be fine after a good night's sleep.'

'I certainly hope so.'

For an instant, Sophie thought Oliver was going to kiss her. She half wished he would, but instead he turned and walked off, calling casually over his shoulder to her, 'Take care, Agnes Wishart. May the force be with you! See you tomorrow.'

Sophie's flat was a thin slice, from front to back, on the first floor of an attractive, south-facing Victorian house built of stone. The solid wooden front door was painted dark blue, with brass fittings, and all the windows had tiny, ornate, wrought-iron balcony surrounds.

Her self-contained, fully-furnished portion consisted of a reasonable sized bed-sitting-room, together with a tiny kitchen and bathroom, but she loved it. This was the first time in her whole life she'd ever lived alone and, far from being lonely, Sophie revelled in its intimacy and particularly the opportunity to shut out the rest of the world. Of course, there were other tenants, who smiled if they passed on the stairs, but that was as far as it went, which was fine by Sophie.

Apart from the privacy, it was the view from the sitting-room's two tall, quarter-paned, rectangular sash-windows across a beautiful park which had totally sold her the idea of the flat — perhaps because it reminded her of the countryside around her parents' country home. On her side of the park there was a formal garden with a lake and waterfalls, but beyond was open parkland and dense woods, inhabited by squirrels and deer.

Sophie loved the view of the park so much, especially when she woke to find it bathed in sunshine, that she'd got into the habit of rarely closing the curtains.

After a shower, Sophie, in a lavender towelling robe, curled up in her favourite armchair beside the window, sipping a mug of hot chocolate. She couldn't help wondering how much longer this blissful state could last. Knowing that Carl might be out there spying on her, she'd been tempted to draw the curtains but, in a curious way, she felt she would far rather be aware of what was going on out there than simply try to blot everything out. She'd done that too often in the past: buried her head in the sand to avoid seeing the truth. She'd ignored all the danger signs. Just as, during stormy rows with her parents when she started seeing Carl, she'd brushed aside their arguments.

When they'd first met, Carl's dog-like devotion to her was very flattering. What girl wouldn't be flattered if the man of her dreams wanted to spend his every free minute with her? It was too late when she realized everything was the other way round: the only reason Carl wanted her constantly beside him was simply so he could check up on her every move.

If she was only minutes late meeting him, there were long cross-examinations. Where had she been? Who with? And when she told him the truth, that the bus was delayed, he'd accused her of lying. Even then, apart from being too proud to admit she'd been wrong, Sophie convinced herself things would improve between them.

When they'd first met, Carl would rarely appear without some small present. He'd always passed compliments about her hair, the way she walked, or simply said what attractive clothes she wore.

But that had quickly changed.

There were no more presents, and when she made herself look presentable he accused her of dolling herself up like a tart to pick up some man he was convinced she fancied.

The point of no return was reached over a Christmas party. They were both invited, but Carl refused to go. Sophie, convinced he'd change his mind, went ahead and bought a really nice long black dress with a split up the leg, the first new one she'd had for ages. But on the night of the party, when Sophie went to Carl's flat to change, she found to her horror that Carl had hacked and slashed the new dress to ribbons with a carving knife. That was when Sophie finally recognized that the only emotion Carl held for her was not love, but an insanely dangerous, uncontrollable jealousy.

Though it had long been simmering beneath the surface of their relationship, the knife episode was the first time Carl's violence had actually erupted. In the weeks which followed, it became an increasing part of everyday life, although Carl was always careful not to leave marks on her face or arms, where they would show.

The end of their relationship was swift and sudden. Though the idea of fourteen days, alone with Carl, terrified her, he'd forced her to agree to a fortnight's holiday in Spain. From the beginning it was horrendous. He refused to let her buy any new clothes to take with her, or even allow her to pack the best of what she'd got. However, the fact that he hid her bikini didn't bother Sophie in the slightest; her body had far too many discoloured bruises for her to want to wear it.

While they were away, when they weren't shouting at each other Carl spent most of his time drinking. They'd been there for six days when, very drunk, Carl gave her the most vicious beating ever. He'd accused her of trying to get off with two Spanish boys, who'd simply been kind enough to give her a lift home after she'd got lost in town during a solitary window-shopping expedition.

Sophie decided it had got to stop. She waited until Carl fell into a drunken sleep and then, taking nothing but her airline ticket, her passport and what little money she had, she fled.

When she reached the airport, they refused to change the date of her flight home. She knew hitch-hiking was dangerous, but she seriously thought, after what Carl had done, nothing worse could happen to her.

Over the next four days she slept rough, slowly making her way up through Spain to France until, eventually, with her last traveller's cheque, she bought a ferry ticket to Dover. Desperate to keep ahead of Carl, she raced home, collected a few belongings, and left town, begging her parents not to tell Carl where she'd gone. It seemed impossible that that was only four months ago. But now, just when she was begin-ning to settle into a proper life, with friends and outside interests, the spectre of Carl had loomed up again.

Should she, once more, pack up and go? No, of course not. She couldn't keep on running for ever. If Carl had tracked her down once, he could as easily do it again. Besides, if he attacked her now, there would almost certainly be witnesses. Sophie shuddered. She knew Carl was far too clever to be caught out like that. Like a cobra, he would bide his time. Revenge was one of his few pleasures and he would savour it. When Carl struck, she was sure it would be vicious and final.

While she'd been thinking, a thick skin had formed over her chocolate. She considered making some more, but decided not to bother. As she got up to go to bed, a movement across the road, in the park, caught her eye.

Sophie quickly snapped out her bedside lamp, the only light in the room, and crept back to the window, to peer round the edge of the open curtain. Had it been her imagination, or merely the breeze stirring one of the branches?

All was still. In the yellow glow of the streetlight, which spilled over into the fringes of the park, nothing moved. Then a branch twitched and, behind it, Sophie could just make out a face lurking in the shadows. Though too dark and too far away to identify features, Sophie was convinced it was Carl.

Deep inside her Sophie knew, locked in her flat, she was perfectly safe, but she didn't feel that way. Hardly daring to breathe, she stared out of the darkened room like a rabbit which becomes transfixed by the beam of a car's headlights. Only after the branch had dropped back into place, and the shadowy figure had slunk off into the depths of the park, did Sophie run for her bed, hiding her head under the duvet, shivering with fear and silently sobbing.

When Sophie finally got to sleep, she kept waking, trembling and bathed in a cold sweat, from a recurring nightmare about the dress Carl had slashed up to stop her going to the Christmas party. The awful part about the dream was, she'd actually been wearing the dress when Carl attacked it with the carving knife and she had ended up hacked to bloody ribbons too. Even awake, the image of her standing, helpless, in a pool of her own blood, with strips of her torn flesh hanging out through the gaping rips in the dress, refused to go away.

Three

By the following day Sophie was exhausted from lack of sleep. Worse, everywhere she went, either going to or from work, when she popped out for lunch, or even in the office itself, Sophie kept imagining she'd caught sight of Carl.

Being kept in a constant state of alert left her extremely edgy. She made stupid mistakes in her own work and then snapped at poor Jimmy, from the post-room, simply because he dropped a wrong letter on her desk.

Paula was quick to notice Sophie's sudden change of mood. 'What on earth's the matter? You're jumpy as a frog and you look awful!'

'Thanks a lot! I feel much better for knowing that!'

Sophie knew telling Paula wouldn't solve anything. During the time she'd spent with Carl, Sophie had never complained to a soul about what he was doing to her — not even to her parents, not until after she'd escaped from him. That had been her last remaining scrap of pride. She'd got herself into the mess; she had to get herself out, unaided. Running to others for help was just not part of Sophie's character.

The best Sophie could hope for now, was that Carl, having found her, might be content to merely torment her for a while, and then go away and leave her alone — though she knew in her heart, that wasn't very likely. That wasn't Carl's way. Having torn the wings off a butterfly, Carl would always, eventually, put the tortured body out of its misery.

By tea-time, having spent all day glancing over her shoulder and trying never to be alone for a second, Sophie was so relieved to get back to the safety of her flat unscathed, she decided to miss rehearsal. She just couldn't face the idea of going out in the dark and walking to the Mill alone. She excused herself on the grounds that her time would be better spent working on her costumes. Apart from the plain shift, a full-length white nightdress, in which she was tortured and then dragged before the court, there was also a dress, and she hadn't started either.

Sophie made herself a peanut butter sandwich, but couldn't bring herself to eat it. Feeling she would go crazy if she didn't talk to someone, she picked up the phone and dialled, hoping she might get her father. Her mother answered.

'Mum, you remember I particularly asked you not to tell Carl my new address?'

'Yes, dear, and we haven't. We've never had the chance. We've seen nothing of him, I'm happy to say.'

'Well, he's found out somehow.'

'Oh dear!'

'Last night he sent me a threatening, anonymous note, and later on I'm sure he was in the park, spying on my flat.'

'Are you certain it's Carl?'

'Mum! How many enemies do you think I've got? Of course it's Carl.'

When Sophie heard her mother sigh, she mentally flinched, awaiting the inevitable lecture.

'Your father and I did warn you what would happen if you got involved with that young man.'

Sophie feebly tried to stem the oncoming tide. 'Yes, I know. . .'

But her mother never missed a chance to rub salt into Sophie's wounds. 'We tried to tell you what sort of a person he was, but you refused to listen to us. Well, I hope you're satisfied now! When I think of the boys you could have gone out with, like David.'

Sophie pulled a face. David was a real nerd, a boy Sophie wouldn't have walked to the nearest palm tree with if they'd been left alone for ten years on a desert island!

'Instead of which, you've thrown your life away over a wastrel like Carl.' Sophie's mother made his name curl down the telephone like a snake. 'Not to mention having to leave that lovely job your father arranged for you. . .'

Sophie broke in. 'Mum! I'm frightened.'

'I'm not surprised. I'd be frightened if I was involved with a psychopath.'

'But what can I do?'

In the brief pause which followed, Sophie visualized the smug look spreading across her mother's face like syrup. Sophie's mother didn't so much *offer* advice, as hack it into tablets of stone, which she then hurled at people.

'Now, when it's too late, you finally come to me for advice!'

Sophie knew it was playing into her hands, but there was no hiding it, she was every bit as desperate as she sounded. 'I don't know what to do and I'm terrified.'

'You should come home,' Sophie's mother said, her voice ringing with triumph. 'None of this would have happened if you hadn't left home in the first place. Daddy might even be able to get you your old job back.'

'Mum, you know I can't do that.'

'That's your trouble. You ask for advice, but never take it when it's given!'

'But coming home would only make things worse. Carl would follow me back and it'd start all over again!'

'Then you've no alternative but to go to the police.'

'And tell them what exactly?'

'That you're being attacked.'

'But that's the whole point, Mum, I'm not. Not yet anyway. It's just a threat. I'm sure he's following me all the time, but there's nothing illegal about that.'

'Show them the letter.'

'It's just a stupid note. They'd probably say it was from some practical joker.'

'Well, perhaps it is,' her mother suggested. 'Maybe how you feel simply comes from you having a terribly guilty conscience over the way you've treated us.'

Sophie had had enough and lied, 'I've got to go, Mum, it's time for rehearsal.'

'And mixing with theatricals won't do you any good,' she sniffed. 'If you'd be ruled by me, you'd have nothing to do with unstable people of that type.'

'You are coming to see the play, aren't you?'

'Well, yes, dear, though it is a long journey for your father.'

'Good, I'll see you then. Bye, Mum,' Sophie said firmly.

Replacing the receiver, Sophie couldn't help wondering if her problems in life hadn't been triggered off by her mother. Years of, 'You can't go out without a vest!' and 'There'll be plenty of time for boys when your exams are over!' were bound to take their toll.

At home, Sophie had never been allowed room to make the smallest decisions for herself. Even the simplest thing, like feeling hungry late at night and going to make a sandwich, always provoked a torrent of uncalled-for advice.

'You'll get terrible indigestion, eating so late. You'll get no sleep, wake up tired tomorrow and not be able to concentrate.'

Worst of all was the emotional blackmail, tagged on to the end of every conversation: 'Well, you please yourself, Sophie. It's up to you what you do, but don't come running to me . . .'

Instead of standing her ground, Sophie had always given in, gone without the sandwich and then not slept from hunger pangs. If she'd ever been allowed to get some practice while she was young, of making her own choices and having to accept their success or failure, learning by experience, then perhaps she wouldn't have made such a stubborn, gross mistake over her first major choice – Carl.

Sophie sometimes felt she was like one of the potted plants her mother was always fussing over. Only in Sophie's case, her mother had protected her too long from the sun, allowing her to grow long and leggy, but with no real strength. Carl's treatment, whilst being the opposite, a harsh mixture of rough handling and neglect, had been no better.

Sophie was convinced, if it hadn't been for her mother's domineering personality, she wouldn't naturally gravitate towards people who wanted to control her every move. Even Paula. She'd been under Paula's thumb from the moment they'd met. Though hers was a kindlier thumb than most and a long way from smother love. Why was it that just as she'd finally found herself the perfect combination of everything, Carl had to come along to uproot her again?

A sudden harsh clattering from the buzzer above her door jerked Sophie out of her thoughts. In all the time she'd lived there, this was the first time anybody had used her doorbell.

It must be Carl.

Sophie crept over to the window. She flattened her face against the wall and tentatively peered out from behind the curtains, through the wrought-iron balustrade and down towards the steps. To her enormous relief she saw not the slight but threatening hunched shoulders of Carl, but the far bulkier ones of Oliver.

When Oliver glanced up and spotted her, he must have thought she'd flipped. Sophie raced down the stairs two at a time and, almost before she'd unlocked the door, began burbling a feeble excuse for her strange behaviour. 'I thought you were going to be someone else.'

'So did I, once,' Oliver said, completely deadpan, 'but this was the way I turned out!' He leaned casually against the door and raised a bewildered eyebrow.

27

Sophie laughed. She suddenly felt much better now that Oliver was there. 'Oh, you know what I mean!'

'More or less. Hey, you were so jumpy last night, I thought I'd come and collect you for rehearsal, just in case you decided not to go.'

A mind-reader on top of everything else. 'Do you want to come up while I get my coat?'

'Nice flat you've got,' he said, glancing round until his eye lit on the untouched sandwich. 'Is this your tea?'

The words had echoes of her mother in them, just after finding the spinach Sophie had left, but the tone was much less critical. 'I wasn't very hungry,' Sophie apologized, as she bent to check her make-up in the dressing-table mirror.

'You really should eat. Have you got a polythene bag or something? Then you could take it with you, in case you suddenly feel hungry during rehearsal.'

How was it Oliver, unlike so many others in her life, managed to say things like that, without making them sound in the least bit fussy or bossy? 'Yes, you'll find a roll of sandwich bags in the drawer of the kitchen sink-unit.'

Sophie was applying fresh lipstick when, over her shoulder, she caught sight of Oliver's reflection in the mirror. Returning from the kitchen, he was rapidly advancing towards her, a bagged sandwich in one hand, but the other clutched the only long, sharp knife she possessed. Sophie swung round. Had Carl some-how persuaded Oliver to do the deed for him?

Seeing the horrified look on Sophie's face, Oliver collapsed in laughter. 'I don't know what you thought I had in mind,' he apologized, 'but I've just noticed this long thread trailing from my sweater sleeve. Would you chop it off for me?' he said, carefully offering her the knife handle.

Sophie's hand trembled so badly, she almost dropped the knife. 'Look,' she suggested, 'if you'd rather have the thread cut off, instead of your hand, I think I'd be safer using nail-scissors.' Even with those, Sophie found it difficult to stop herself shaking long enough to catch hold of the thread and remove it.

'Sophie, I wish you'd tell me what's upsetting you,' Oliver said, his voice full of concern.

'I'm being silly, that's all,' she said over-brightly, and, carelessly stuffing the sandwich into her bag, she headed for the door. 'Come on, or we'll be late.'

Rehearsal went very well until Oliver and Sophie got a fit of giggles. It started in the silliest way, when Oliver pulled a stupid face to cheer her up. Probably because she'd been living on her nerves all day, it worked too well and made Sophie collapse. Normally that would have been the end of it but, after that, they only had to catch each other's eye to burst into more fits of laughter.

At *any* time during the tragedy of Agnes Wishart's life their laughter wouldn't have helped. But it couldn't have been less appropriate than in the courtroom scene, when Julian, as the Magistrate, was severely criticizing Hopkins for using the procedure of waking-and-walking in order to obtain a confession from Agnes.

MAGISTRATE: I have heard, from them that watched with her, that you kept this girl awake continuously for several nights and ran her backwards and forwards across the cell. Then, after a short rest, you did it again. This was repeated over several days and nights till the girl was weary of life and scarce sensible of what she did or said. I have to ask you, Mathew Hopkins, if you believe this to be fit procedure?

MATHEW: [*Strutting across to the Magistrate*] The Bible is my guide. [*He holds a copy aloft*] Exodus, chapter twenty-two, verse eighteen, states: 'Thou shalt not suffer a witch to live'.

MAGISTRATE: Mr Hopkins, I can assure you I am very familiar with the scripture to which you refer.

MATHEW: Then, as Magistrate of this town, I would have thought your duty was clear. Rather than seek to criticize me and my tried and tested methods, your sole concern should be to assist me in persecuting the Devil, of which this miserable woman is the vessel. If you do not, we would be forced . . .

But once again Oliver caught Sophie's eye and burst out laughing. This time, Nathan's normally inexhaustible supply of patience ran out and, hurling his script to the floor, he screamed, 'I can't work like this! If you'd rather do *Noddy in Toyland*, just say so!'

There was a second's stunned silence before Oliver, in an imitation of a child's voice, said loudly, 'So!'

The tension broken, the whole cast collapsed in laughter, until even Nathan was forced to join in.

After everyone had sobered up, Oliver apologized properly. 'Honestly, Nathan, I promise you, we're not doing it on purpose. We can't help ourselves.'

'OK,' Nathan said, 'let's take an early coffee break and I just hope, when you come back, you'll be in a more sensible frame of mind. I must remind you this production goes on in two weeks, and it's far from ready!'

There was a general murmur of apprehension as they filed out towards the green-room, which was in the cellar beneath the dressing-rooms, reached by using the lower part of a narrow, wooden staircase. The flight continued upwards, right to the top of the building, twisting continually at right angles, hugging the dusty, outside walls of a square tower, leaving a well in the centre.

Its banister rails had been polished smooth by the rough hands of generations of workmen, but the steps above stage level were uneven, having been worn down by the constant tread of their hobnailed boots. Only from the stage down, for the sake of safety, and quiet during performances, had the steps been carpeted.

Curiously, even on the warmest day, it was impossible to use the staircase without being aware of a searing, cold draught, sucked straight down the tower, like a fiendish wind, fresh from the Arctic.

During the break, to make everyone feel more guilty,

Nathan inquired loudly, 'How are your costumes coming along? Don't forget, first dress rehearsal's only ten days away! I think we should start seeing the results before that. We don't want to leave everything to the last minute, do we?'

Sophie whispered to Paula, 'I've hardly started either of mine!'

'Me neither,' Paula admitted.

'I never was good at sewing, and doing it by hand takes for ever!'

'I tell you what,' Paula suggested. 'Why don't we come here at the weekend? There are two sewing-machines and it would be so much quicker.'

'Good idea,' agreed Sophie.

'I think it's sexist,' Celia protested, 'the men having their costumes hired, while the women have to make theirs.'

But Nathan had moved on. 'We've also got to finish the skull masks for the chorus. Tim's made us some excellent wire frames, but covering those will have to be a joint effort.'

'Thank goodness we don't have any scenery to paint as well!' Paula muttered under her breath.

Because the production was being done in the round, the settings consisted of a few rostra and items of furniture, which the cast themselves moved around as part of the action. Tim, having only a couple of small parts, had volunteered to be the stage-manager and make any small props he couldn't borrow from local people.

Before Nathan could find any more jobs for them, Angie cut in. 'Nathan, when are we going to get round to sorting out the final act?'

The last scene had been a bone of contention for several weeks. Some of the cast wanted to stick purely with the story of Agnes, ending with the suitor's deathbed confession, after the death of Agnes. Others felt the play needed an epilogue, to include something about the repeal of the Witchcraft Law in 1712, but which also mentioned that the last British witch was drowned during the nineteenth century.

Either way, Nathan had constantly avoided the issue and always looked uncomfortable when the subject was raised. 'I haven't forgotten, but I'm still thinking it through,' he said, scowling at the floor.

Andrew, a shortish young man with a balding head and a straggly beard, who was very good in the play as Sophie's distraught father, came to Nathan's rescue. 'Something more immediate than that,' he called out, waving a roll of papers at them. 'I picked up the posters from the printer today.'

'Oh, let's have a look,' Paula said eagerly.

'You'll have plenty of chances to look at them,' Andrew said. 'I hope you've all remembered — months ago you happily agreed to take some each and distribute them around the town?' There were some mild groans. 'It's too late to moan now!'

Nathan offered his support. 'No publicity means no audience, and all the work we've put in would be wasted.'

'Look,' Andrew said, 'I don't mind going round with a bucket of glue and doing all the fly-posting, but we also need to persuade people to hang them up in as many shops, offices and house windows as possible, and there are far too many for me to cope with on my own. To avoid wasted effort and everybody pestering the same shopkeepers, I've divided up the town between you. I'll give you some posters and a photostatted map with your area marked on it.'

'What if we have any left over?' little Angie piped up.

'Just use them up wherever you think best. I mean, if you go to a club which you know none of the rest of us use, it doesn't matter whether it's in your segment or not, does it?'

As Andrew cut the string and smoothed out the roll, everyone gathered round to look over his shoulder. The design was simple but effective: all in black, on white paper. The lower half was filled with a list of performers, followed by details of the ticket prices and where to obtain them.

The really eye-catching part of the design was the top half. Beneath the name of the theatre and the title of the play done in bold letters, was a strikingly detailed pen and ink drawing of the figure of Agnes Wishart. One of her hands reached out, pathetically imploring her unseen tormentors for mercy.

Andrew divided the posters up amongst the cast. When he came to Sophie he said, 'I've given you a few extra because you've got the centre of town, where there are more opportunities close together.'

Sophie was so relieved not to have to wander alone around some strange, remote part of town, she didn't mind at all. 'Yes, that's fine. They're very good, aren't they?'

Andrew smiled. 'Credit for that goes to Oliver. He did the layout and all the artwork.'

Either by accident or design (Sophie couldn't help noticing and feeling rather flattered), the face in

Oliver's drawing was more a portrait of her than of Agnes.

'Come on, everyone!' Nathan called out. 'We must get on, otherwise there won't be a production to advertise!'

Sophie was about to follow the others out of the green-room when, just as Oliver had predicted, she realized she was beginning to feel hungry and reached into her bag. During rehearsal she'd left her bag beside the fridge, but when she felt inside, the sandwich wasn't there.

Positive she'd brought it, Sophie dumped the entire contents on the floor, but still there was no sign of the sandwich, or even the plastic bag Oliver had wrapped it in.

How odd, she thought. Surely none of the cast could be so desperate they needed to steal a perfectly ordinary peanut butter sandwich?

'Sophie!' Nathan yelled from the acting area. 'We're waiting for you!'

She hastily scooped everything back into her bag and was about to run up the steps, when she was suddenly aware that the usual cold blast of air was this time accompanied by a tremendous banging above her. Instinctively, Sophie jumped back and, a split second later, screamed, as a torrent of bricks and masonry hurtled down the stairwell, to crash at her feet in a cloud of dust.

Four

Sophie stood, frozen, staring at the pile which lay at her feet: six heavy old bricks, some smashed to fragments by the force of the impact. When she looked up, she found herself surrounded by concerned people, all asking questions.

'Are you all right?' asked Angie, cautiously reaching out to touch the banister where it had been splintered as one of the bricks smashed into it. 'You could easily have been killed!'

'Shouldn't you sit down?' Andrew asked. 'You look terribly pale.'

'I think that's mostly dust,' Sophie said. Though as she carelessly brushed a hand over her face, she felt herself swaying uncertainly.

During that moment of wooziness, she spotted Oliver. For some strange reason, he appeared to be standing on the stairs high above the others, though he quickly pushed his way through the throng and took her hand. 'Your arm's bleeding.'

Sophie, resisting the temptation to pull away from him, looked blankly at the trickle of blood oozing from the painful graze. 'I suppose one of the bricks must have caught it. Everything happened so quickly, I didn't notice at the time.'

'They can only have missed you by a hair's breadth,' Oliver said.

Sophie, still wondering what he'd been doing upstairs, couldn't help thinking he'd known that all along.

Nathan towered over her and nervously thrust his glasses back into place. 'What exactly happened?'

Still wondering what Oliver had been up to and suffering slightly from delayed shock, Sophie shook her head weakly. 'I don't really know. I'd just left the green-room, when I heard a noise above me. I'd only just stepped back when . . .' Sophie broke off and waved a trembling hand at the broken bricks.

Angie, looking very serious, said quietly, 'I think it's meant as a warning.'

Sophie looked startled. 'What do you mean by that?' Sophie's own thoughts had been along similar lines. Until she'd caught sight of Oliver coming downstairs, her immediate suspicion had been that it was Carl who had somehow managed to send the pile of bricks crashing down on top of her, as a prelude to his revenge. But how could Angie possibly know about Carl?

It turned out the warning Angie had in mind was from a totally different source. 'I've said all along how dangerous it is to dabble in witchcraft!'

Several people who'd heard Angie's opinions before smiled tolerantly, but Nathan jumped on her. 'Angie, that's nonsense! We aren't dabbling in it. If anything our story's against the whole idea of the existence of witches.'

Angie wasn't convinced. 'But that's my point! This is exactly the kind of inexplicable thing that starts happening when people interfere in matters they don't understand!'

'I certainly think,' Nathan said firmly, 'it's very dangerous to draw conclusions from coincidental events.'

But Angie wasn't to be put off. 'Is it a coincidence that Sophie was the thirteenth person to join the company?'

'There are still only twelve actors,' Pete pointed out.

'But thirteen in the company, if you include Nathan,' Angie counted.

'Or fourteen,' Nathan said, 'if you count Eddie.'

Angie refused to budge from her version. 'He's only the caretaker and quite separate from the company performing the play. All I'm saying is Sophie was the thirteenth person to join and nothing like this ever happened until she joined.'

'So you think I'm some sort of curse?' Sophie asked.

While others laughed, Angie, in all seriousness, said, 'You can scoff, but you know as well as I do, everybody always avoids sitting down thirteen to a table!'

'I've never heard such nonsense,' Nathan said, but before he could further attack Angie's argument he was interrupted by Eddie, who'd just returned from the pub. 'What's been going on here?' Nathan quickly explained and Eddie shook his head. 'It'll be those damned rooks again!'

Nathan found Eddie's explanation even more unlikely than Angie's. 'Rooks don't fly round hurling down bricks like bombers!'

'But they are harbingers of evil,' Angie said smugly.

From early childhood, Sophie had always been terrified of birds, particularly large black ones. Though her father had constantly assured her it was impossible, Sophie had always feared that birds, or bats, might somehow get entangled in her hair. Just the thought of their claws clutching and scratching at her was enough to make her scalp prickle, as if a thousand insects were running over it.

But Eddie, a middle-aged, wiry man and practical to his core, swivelled his cold, grey eyes round on to Angie and then ignored her. 'Rooks root about in the roof space, building their nests and dislodging the old masonry, until eventually some topples out. I spend half me time clearing up their mess and repairing the damage they do. It's happened a time or two up on the top floor, but I'd never realized they'd got in above the staircase. If I had my way, I'd shoot the blessed things.'

Angie was outraged. 'You can't do that! If they deserted the Mill, terrible things would happen!'

'I think, Angie,' Nathan said patiently, 'you're getting confused. That's if the *ravens* ever leave the Tower of London!'

Angie coloured slightly, but stood her ground. 'Well, it's the same sort of thing.'

Nathan had had enough. 'Angie, perhaps you could go and make Sophie a cup of strong tea?'

'I'm sorry this happened,' Eddie said to Sophie. 'You all keep out of the way for a bit. I'll clear up the mess later. But first I want to go up and make sure there's nothing else loose that can fall.'

Eddie's receding footsteps echoed in the tower

above them, as Nathan began to organize everybody. 'Sophie, we'll manage without you for now. Go and have a sit down in the green-room until you feel better.'

'I'm fine, honestly,' Sophie insisted.

'Well, I think you should at least drink the tea Angie's making you first,' Nathan said.

'And that cut needs attention,' Oliver pointed out. 'I'll clean it up for you.'

Sophie, uncertain now as to whether he'd really been coming down the stairs after the accident or not, for the time being felt she didn't want Oliver to touch her. 'Let Angie do it,' she said quickly.

'Yes, that would be better,' Nathan agreed. 'We can manage to rehearse without Sophie and Angie for a while, but we can't afford to lose you as well, Oliver.'

Sophie obediently sipped hot, strong, sweet tea, which she hated, while Angie fussed over bathing and bandaging the wound.

'It's a nasty graze.'

Sophie shrugged. 'It might have been a really nasty accident.'

Angie fixed her with a stern look. 'If it was an accident!'

'Oh, come on, Angie, you surely don't believe all that superstitious stuff, do you?'

Sophie still secretly believed that Carl was a far more likely explanation than supernatural forces. And if not Carl, perhaps Oliver? Though she had no idea why Oliver would want to do such a dreadful thing to her.

'Believe me,' said Angie, 'strange things do happen. Did you know this mill is haunted?'

'Really?'

Angie gave a knowing nod. 'Oh yes. I wouldn't be surprised if it was the ghost that scared the professional theatre company out of here.'

Sophie didn't think that sounded very likely. 'Have you seen the ghost yourself?'

'No,' Angie admitted reluctantly, 'but while I was doing some research on Agnes, I read about it in the old newspapers in the library, and a lot of the locals already know the story. Some were alive when it started. Apparently the last miller to grind corn here was Seth Garner, and in 1925 he was found, swinging by his neck from the hoist used to haul the grain sacks up to the top floor.'

'He committed suicide?'

'Nobody knew for certain. I suppose somebody could have tied him up and pushed him off, but at the time, most people believed he hanged himself. He was supposed to be a middle-aged bachelor with few friends, although there was some rumour about a girl he knew in the town, but after his death nobody could trace her. Anyway, he didn't leave a note and there never was a proper explanation for what he did.'

'How awful!'

'Yes,' Angie agreed and then dramatically lowered her voice, before adding, with great relish, 'but the really grisly part was his body must have been hanging there for several days because, when they found it, his eyes and tongue had been completely eaten away!'

Sophie shuddered. 'Ugh! That's terrible.'

But Angie was relishing telling her story so much, she didn't notice the effect it was having on Sophie. 'Some of the locals reckon it was the ancestors of those rooks up there, which pecked his eyes out.' She jerked her thumb up towards the roof. 'Others say it was more likely rats, which climbed down the rope and ate them. But whatever happened, the ghost of Seth Garner still haunts the Mill to this very day!'

Suddenly a man's voice cut abruptly into their conversation. 'I've never heard such rubbish!'

Startled, Sophie and Angie swung round to find Eddie standing in the doorway. They'd been so busy talking, they hadn't heard him come down the stairs, ready to clear away the rubble.

Angie was stung by his remark. 'You can't say it isn't true. I've seen copies of the original newspaper articles myself and talked to old people who were alive when it happened!'

'I bet you have!' Eddie said bitterly. 'There's always folks who like gossip and there's nothing they enjoy more than poking their noses into other people's affairs! I've lived round here all my life too and I've been coming here since I was a lad, but I've never seen no signs of any ghost!'

As Angie flounced past Eddie, she said, 'Say what you like, there's something very strange about this building!'

Sophie asked Eddie, 'Did you find anything up there?'

He shook his head. 'Nothing – only bird-droppings. It was like I said – they shuffle about so much, something's bound to fall, sooner or later. It happens in very old buildings. I'm only glad nothing worse happened to you, young lady.'

'Thanks. I'm fine now, honestly.'

'There was one strange thing though,' Eddie said, rubbing his stubbly chin thoughtfully.

'Oh, what was that?'

'Have any of your lot been messing about up there lately?'

Sophie shrugged. 'Not that I know of. We're usually all down here, together, working. Why?'

'It's just that I haven't been up to the very top for a while. I try to get round regular, but there's too much to do . . .'

'Yes?' Sophie interrupted impatiently.

'Well, when I went up there just now, the place was covered in dust, as usual, but in the dust I could see a lot of brand-new footprints.'

The frightening thought flashed into Sophie's mind, those footprints could easily belong to Carl. While they were all busy on stage, rehearsing, he could have sneaked into the building without being spotted.

Then a cold shiver ran down Sophie's spine. The footprints could just as easily be Oliver's — though she still couldn't work out what reason he had to harm her. But what else could he be doing, up in a part of the Mill the group never used? What if, underneath his bumbling, good-looking, kindly exterior, there lurked another, far more sinister Oliver; much more like Mathew Hopkins than he'd been letting on?

Five

Her arm bound up by Angie in far more bandage then was justified, Sophie rejoined the rest of the cast. As she passed Paula, she whispered, 'Will you walk home with me tonight, after rehearsal?'

Paula stifled a laugh. 'This is so sudden!'

'I'm serious!' Sophie hissed.

Sophie's worried expression stifled any further attempt at humour from Paula. 'Why, what's up?'

'I'll tell you later,' said Sophie, and quickly swopped places with Marge, who'd been standing-in for her as Agnes. Or *lying-in* really, for they were working on the beginning of the opening to the torture scene in which Sophie had to lie still, stretched out on a table, while Mathew Hopkins demonstrated his evil skills to his newly-recruited assistant John, played by Shaun.

Though it was a scene she normally enjoyed, for once it brought Sophie far closer to Oliver than she wanted to be.

MATHEW: First we will seek the witch-mark on her.

[*Mathew examines Agnes in minute detail; from the soles of her feet to the crown of her head*]

MATHEW: Seek out the slightest blemish. Any spot or tiny mark would do. See, here's one for us to test.

[*He points to a mole on Agnes's left arm and, from his bag, produces a fiendish, long brass needle set in a black jet handle, which looks like a miniature dagger*]

MATHEW: Most witches may be proved guilty by the witch-mark alone. For it is a mark left by the Devil, and when they are pricked on it witches neither cry out nor bleed.

[*Mathew, in a single thrust, drives half the needle deep into the flesh of her arm before withdrawing it equally swiftly. Agnes neither flinches nor appears to experience the slightest pain. She remains perfectly still and quiet, as if nothing had happened*]

MATHEW: [*Examines the result and cries out in triumph*] See! There is no blood! Though you saw me drive the needle deep into her flesh, there is no blood on the needle and it left barely a mark on her evil skin. Nor did she cry out with pain, as you or I would. Surely a true indication of a witch!

[*Mathew Hopkins and John continue their examination of Agnes in silence while the Narrator addresses the audience*]

NARRATOR: They can find no mark because there is

45

none. Nor could there be, for the needle witch-prickers used was as false as is my dagger.

[*The Narrator walks across to Agnes and, gripping the handle of a dagger in both hands, raises it high above her before appearing to plunge it, viciously, into her stomach. Still Agnes does not move or make any sound*]

NARRATOR: And the reason she shows no mark, nor makes any sound, is because the dagger is a trick one. The same kind children still use for their games.

[*The Narrator demonstrates by putting his fingertip to the point of the blade and pushing, until the whole blade disappears into the handle*]

NARRATOR: But though Mathew Hopkins's game had a more evil purpose, his needle is as tricky as my dagger. And if its point should leave the tiniest mark, it would be easily hidden by whichever blemish he tested. But although the needle was a trick, the outcome still meant death to his innocent victims. For this method was widely accepted as total proof of guilt. But even if it were not, Hopkins kept an armoury full of other methods. Many of these were far more genuine when it came to breaking down protestations of innocence and securing a willing confession of guilt from his victims. If only to persuade him to stop.

JOHN: Shall you leave it there, Master? Will
            the witch-mark be sufficient proof?

MATHEW: Ordinarily, yes. But this particular witch
            is so alluring, there may be doubts in
            court. To alleviate that risk, and because
            it will give me a chance to exhibit more
            of my gentle persuaders, we will test
            this pretty witch a little further. Heat up
            these iron leg-frames over the brazier!

'Hold it!' Nathan said, coming from the auditorium
into the acting area to give the actors notes on their
performances. 'Oliver, when you first produce the
needle it's very small. So do it as if you were bringing
a rabbit out of a hat. Take your time. Get more nasty
pleasure into it.' Nathan showed him how. 'And remember, we're working in the round. Hold the needle up
high above your head, like a sword. You'll be in a
circle of light from a single spot and I want the needle
to glint so we can all see how awful it looks.'

Oliver repeated the action with a particularly evil
leer.

'That's it!' Nathan was delighted by Oliver's performance. But, since the accident and Eddie's discovery of
the footprints on the top floor, Sophie was not so
thrilled. She had been so easily taken in by first
appearances with Carl, she no longer trusted her
judgement now about Oliver.

'What has suddenly gone wrong between you and
Oliver?' Paula demanded, the moment they'd left the
Mill.

Paula hadn't failed to notice how Sophie had

suddenly started avoiding Oliver during the rest of rehearsal and, when it ended, abruptly refused his usual, friendly invitation to go for coffee.

Sophie half-ignored the question. 'Before I answer, you tell me something. Just before the bricks came down on me, where was Oliver?'

Paula was baffled. 'What?'

'It's important,' Sophie insisted. 'I need to know.'

'OK, take it easy! Let me think. We'd all just gone up after coffee, hadn't we? I'm fairly sure we were all together.'

But that wasn't good enough for Sophie. 'Are you positive?'

'Yes, I am!' Paula said. 'Come to think of it, he must have been one of the first up there, because when I arrived he was swinging from the iron ladder — you know, the one that runs straight up the wall beside the entrance from the foyer?'

'Swinging from it?'

'That's right,' Paula nodded. 'He was fooling about, pretending to be Tarzan, or Cheetah. What is all this about, Sophie?'

Sophie took a deep breath. 'After the bricks fell, Eddie went upstairs to check round and he found recent footprints in the dust.'

'And what's that got to do with Oliver?'

'Well, just after the bricks missed me, while I was still recovering from the shock, I could have sworn I saw Oliver coming down the stairs.'

'He'd have to, from the stage,' Paula pointed out, 'we all did.'

'No,' Sophie insisted, 'I'm certain Oliver came from higher up the stairs than the rest of you.'

Paula suddenly realized the point Sophie was making and was amazed. 'You mean you think Oliver had something to do with those bricks falling?'

'Not just "something to do with",' said Sophie carefully. 'If Oliver *was* up there he could actually have caused the accident!'

'But why on earth would he want to do that, to you of all people? The guy's crazy about you!'

Sophie wasn't comfortable about Paula's use of the word crazy, but she let it pass. 'Is he?'

There was no doubt in Paula's mind. 'You were too busy turning your back on him at the end of rehearsal! Otherwise you'd have seen how hurt and puzzled he looked when you refused his invitation to go for coffee.'

Sophie sighed. 'Oh, I don't know. Maybe I'm wrong about the whole thing.'

By the look on Paula's face she obviously thought so. She didn't reply and they had walked for quite a while, in silence, before she said, 'I've known Oliver for a long time and I'm positive he's not the sort of person to hurt a fly, much less a human being!'

'But how much do you really know about him? He never talks about friends, or his family.'

'True,' Paula agreed. 'But nor do you! I still think I know enough about Oliver to be positive he wouldn't try to kill anyone and especially not you. Sophie, in all the time I've known Oliver you're the first girl he's ever shown any real interest in, and that's not from any lack of trying on the part of other girls! Believe me, there was a long queue ahead of you. Including some who would have willingly donated parts of their body, and thought it a cheap price to pay, purely for the pleasure of getting their hooks into him!'

'And he never went out with any of them?'

'Not that I know of. You're the only girl I've ever seen him alone with, and now you're accusing him of trying to kill you! It doesn't add up!'

When they reached the pool of light outside Sophie's home, she turned to face Paula. 'Look, forget everything I've said. I'm probably just upset by what happened.'

'That's understandable.' Paula smiled. 'It would have scared me too!'

'Would you like to come in for coffee?'

'Some other time. To be honest, Nathan's made me feel extremely guilty about my costume, or the lack of it. I'm going to go straight home and make a start.'

'But wouldn't it be much quicker to use the sewing-machines at the Mill?'

'Yes,' Paula agreed. 'But I've still got to cut it out. I was going to go in on Saturday morning to sew it up.'

'Could I still come with you?' Sophie almost pleaded. She needed as many allies as possible and was anxious to know she hadn't lost Paula's friendship because of her accusations against Oliver.

'Sure,' Paula said with a smile. 'A Saturday Morning Sewing Circle; it's a date! See you!'

But as Sophie unlocked the door to her flat, she remembered the fright Oliver had given her earlier that evening, when he'd come into the room behind her clutching the knife.

Of course, he'd given a perfectly innocent explanation for that and maybe there was a similar one for him being on the staircase when the bricks fell but, until she knew it, Sophie still thought she might be safer not risking Oliver's protection.

Next evening, to avoid being collected by Oliver after work, Sophie bought a hamburger and went straight to rehearsal.

When he arrived late, having called round at Sophie's, Oliver still seemed as if he couldn't understand why Sophie was avoiding him. But, as Sophie told herself, his air of injured innocence could all be part of the act. After all, from his excellent performance as Mathew Hopkins, Oliver was a very good actor.

However, that evening nothing unusual happened, until Nathan called for a coffee-break.

'There isn't any,' little Angie piped up.

Nathan looked puzzled. 'Isn't any what?'

'Coffee,' Angie replied. 'It's all gone.'

'It can't have,' Paula said. 'I bought a new jar two nights ago.'

Angie nodded. 'I know, I saw you put it in the green-room cupboard, along with the tea, but neither of them is there now and most of the sugar's gone too.'

To satisfy everyone's curiosity, they all trooped out into the green-room, only to discover that for once Angie wasn't making anything up.

Paula opened the fridge. 'I put a two-litre bottle of milk in here last night as well, but it's more than half empty already.'

Nathan took charge. 'People must have been helping themselves to extra cups rather more than usual.'

'But there's something else,' Angie said. 'I brought a Snickers bar with me tonight, to have with coffee, and it's disappeared from my bag.'

'Funnily enough,' Marge agreed, 'the same sort of thing happened to me a couple of nights back, only it was apples.'

51

Sophie said, 'And my peanut butter sandwich disappeared last night.'

'Could be rats,' Andrew suggested. 'There's enough of them about!'

'Oh, come on!' Paula said doubtfully. 'Rats don't normally eat the wrapping as well as the food.'

'They might have carried it off to use as nest material,' Andrew said defensively.

'And I suppose,' Paula said scornfully, 'it was a rat that climbed into the cupboard, opened the coffee jar and then screwed the lid back on when they'd finished? And it must have been a super-rat that managed to open the fridge door!'

'Yes, you're right,' Andrew agreed.

'I think the rat that's taken the stuff walks on two legs and is human!' Paula said.

Nathan looked worried. 'Which can only mean one of us. I'd hate to think that anyone here ... ' But before Nathan could get any further, everybody was loudly protesting their innocence. He held up his hands for quiet. 'It's all very well everyone saying "it isn't me", but if it isn't one of us, who does that leave? After all, the place is locked up all day.'

'And who locks it up?' Marge said triumphantly. 'Eddie!'

Nathan didn't believe that. 'Oh, come on! Eddie's a nice enough guy. A little weird maybe, but that doesn't mean he steals our stuff. Anyway, if we haven't any coffee, we can't have a break. Let's get back to work!'

Just before ten o'clock on the Saturday morning, Sophie dumped her heavy bag, containing the beginnings of her costumes, on the ground, and leaned against the side of the river bridge. It was the first time she'd ever visited the Mill in daylight. It was a bright, sunny day and she simply couldn't get over how totally different the place looked. No longer remotely forbidding.

The river winked and glinted in the sunlight, and the huge waterwheel stood against brickwork which had been warmed by the sun to a blushing orange-pink. All the scene needed, to make a perfect picture for the kind of old-fashioned calendar her mother loved, was straggling wistaria and rambler roses.

'But where's Paula?' Sophie said, checking her watch.

They'd agreed to meet at ten and spend the whole day in the green-room, working on their costumes. They'd arranged for Eddie to let them in, but now it was gone ten, there was no sign of Paula and, nice as it looked from the outside, Sophie didn't like the idea of going into the Mill alone.

'Oh, there you are,' Eddie called to Sophie, as he walked across the car-park towards her. 'I thought you must have changed your minds.'

'Sorry, Eddie. Paula hasn't arrived yet and I stopped to admire the view.'

Eddie let out a deep sigh of contentment. 'Wonderful sight, isn't it? Oak frame with elm floats, she is!' Eddie said proudly.

Sophie was lost. 'Pardon?'

'That wheel you're admiring,' Eddie said, nodding towards it. 'Built to last for ever.'

Trust a man to suffer from tunnel vision. 'Then why did they need to put a new one in when the mill was restored?'

'Only because it was left standing in one position in the water for years, until it eventually rotted away. Oak and elm will take plenty of wetting, as long as it gets some dry too,' Eddie said. 'That's why I have to turn it regular.'

'I've never seen it moving.'

'You could,' Eddie said, 'if you're about tomorrow. Every Sunday morning, some of the restoration society members come down and I give her a turn.'

'How does the water get to the wheel?'

Eddie pointed to the sluice-gate, set in the bank. Above it was a metal wheel, chained and padlocked so that it wouldn't turn. 'We raise the gate, then the water runs along that wooden trough and falls on the top of the wheel to make it turn. Which is why it's called an overshot wheel.' Eddie warmed to his favourite topic. 'They're far more efficient than an undershot, unless you fit those with curved floats.'

Sophie, hoping not to get bogged down in a morass of technical detail, asked, 'How do you control the speed of the wheel?'

'By the amount of water you let through the sluice. I mean, if the river's in flood, you can't just open the gate and hope for the best. It might run so fast it could smash the machinery to bits!'

'The river's so low at the moment,' Sophie observed, 'it hardly looks as if it could turn the wheel at all.'

'That's down to the dry summer we had, but you wait till the rains come! Mind you, she'll still turn. I tell you what, if you come tomorrow, I could show you over the whole thing, while it's running. Fascinating stuff!'

'Yes, I'm sure,' said Sophie, trying to sound enthusiastic. 'Only I'm not certain what I'm doing tomorrow.'

Determined to change the subject before Eddie got started again, Sophie decided to see if he could throw any light on the mystery of their disappearing supplies. 'Eddie, can anyone get into the Mill without the key?'

'Not unless they're Spiderman! There are no windows on the ground floor and the two entrance doors are solid wood. It'd take a bulldozer to get through them!' he said, admiring his sturdy baby. 'Why do you ask?'

Sophie shuffled uncomfortably. Trying to be subtle, she said, offhandedly, 'It's just that, over the last few days, several items of food and drink have gone from the green-room.'

But as Eddie went bright red, it was obvious she hadn't been subtle enough. 'Well, if it's not one of you lot, that only leaves me and I hope you're not suggesting I took them?'

'Oh, no!' Sophie said quickly.

'But I'm the only one with the key.'

'Yes, but . . .'

'I'm the caretaker, remember, and instead of accusing me, maybe you should ask some of your own. Like whoever it was who went up to the top floor, where they had no business! Anyway, I can't hang around all day! Here you are,' he said, shoving a heavy iron key into Sophie's hand. 'And be sure to lock up properly when you've finished. We don't want anything else going missing, do we?'

'I didn't mean . . .' But it was too late. Eddie was already almost out of earshot. Sophie shouted after him. 'What shall I do with the key afterwards?'

Eddie didn't bother to turn round, but called over his shoulder, 'Drop it in my letter-box. Twenty-six Swan Lane.'

Six

The stage door had barely closed behind Sophie, shutting out the warm, friendly sunlight, before she regretted upsetting Eddie. Apart from him being a nice enough guy, if Paula wasn't going to turn up Sophie would have been glad of anyone's company, even Eddie's. A detailed, guided tour of the Mill's machinery would have been a small price to pay to avoid being left alone in the huge building, which was cold and largely in darkness.

Not knowing where any of the light-switches were, Sophie cautiously left the weak pool of light inside the stage door, and went through the swing-doors into the vast darkness of the theatre. As the doors hissed shut, Sophie was confronted by a black wall of silence, only broken by the occasional sharp cracking of the wooden beams which, in the total quiet, sounded even louder and more like gunshots than usual.

With no working-light, all Sophie had to guide her was a dim glow from the far side of the auditorium, filtering up the stairs from the green-room. Around her the darkness was so intense Sophie felt she could only keep her balance by concentrating on that glow ahead.

Floorboards squeaked beneath Sophie's feet as she slowly eased her way down the aisle, hands reaching out attempting to read the darkness, clutching at the seat backs as she passed the end of each row.

Eventually, Sophie reached the acting area which appeared to have doubled its diameter. As she edged her way across, past vague silhouettes, several times she collided with unexpected lumps of furniture, painfully hacking her shins. The noises from her mistakes turned into echoes, which chased each other round and round the curved walls of the big auditorium until they slowly faded and were absorbed by its emptiness.

After what seemed like an eternity, she arrived at the staircase, but as she walked down, her hand happened to touch the splintered dent in the banister, where the falling brick had caught it. She snatched her hand back as if she'd been bitten. She didn't wish, especially in the half-light, to be reminded of what dreadful things could happen in this building.

As she got closer to the welcoming light spilling out from the green-room, feeling a similar relief to that an astronaut experiences after returning safely from a solo mission in outer space, Sophie sprinted down the last few steps.

By the time she had completed an hour's machining, Sophie's confidence was slowly returning. She'd finished off the plain white shift and was about to tackle the more ornate dress, when she heard someone walking about in the theatre.

She called, 'Is that you, Paula?'

The only response came from a mouse, which scrabbled noisily across the bare boards above her head. Then Sophie distinctly heard another, louder footstep. Whoever it was, they were much closer.

Less hopefully, she called again, 'Paula?'

When she still received no reply, Sophie went to the green-room door and peered out, blinking, trying to quickly adjust her eyes to the gloom.

Sophie tried to hold her voice steady as she called out, 'Who's there?'

A sudden, sharp creak on the stairs immediately above her made Sophie look up. She caught a glimpse of something dark which appeared to be almost floating up the stairs. Memories of Angie's story of Seth Garner suddenly flooded Sophie's mind. Could it be his ghost?

Forcing herself to sound far braver than she felt, Sophie shouted after the departing figure, 'It's no good creeping around! I've seen you!'

Her voice, ricocheting off the tower walls, did the trick. The figure immediately abandoned stealth and began to race up the steps, two and three at a time.

'That's a hell of a noisy ghost!' Sophie said to herself and, realizing it was more likely a thief who'd crept in, she gave chase.

But by the time she arrived, breathless, on the top floor, there was no sign of the intruder, apart from a few smudged footprints, similar to the ones Eddie had described, etched into the grey dust which carpeted the old, bare boards. Motes of more recently disturbed dust still twirled in what weak beams of sunlight could filter through a window in the far wall. Its panes were coated with a layer of grime and curtained with thick nets of dusty cobwebs.

The only other occasional shafts of light came from gaps in the roof where rooks had forced slates aside to find spaces for their nests.

Next to the window on the outer wall was a double-door, held shut by a rusty chain and padlock. Beside the door, the drive shaft came up through a gap in the floor and terminated in a series of large wooden cogs and gear-wheels. Years of wear, powering the sack hoist, had polished their intermeshed teeth smooth.

With a jolt, Sophie realized this was the hoist which had once been Seth Garner's gibbet. A hideous image flashed into her mind of Seth's stiffened, eyeless corpse, hanging by its neck, the body turning slowly as it swung in the wind.

Trying to banish the picture from her mind, Sophie forced herself to concentrate on the reality of her surroundings. The whole, vast floor ran the length and width of the building, but was in two distinct parts.

The largest section was to her left – a broad expanse of floor where, presumably, the sacks of grain were stored whilst waiting to be milled. Apart from the yawning jaw of an open hopper, to feed the grain down towards the millstones, there were only some crumpled, grubby sheets of newspaper and a few wide patches of bird-droppings. The droppings gave an acidic tang to the already mouldy, damp smell which hung in the air.

The smaller bit of the loft, running along the right-hand wall from Sophie to the hoist, was divided up by wooden partitions into a series of offices, or more small storerooms. Most of the dull-green, blistered doors were shut, and Sophie knew any one of them would provide the thief with a perfect hiding-place.

With no other way out, whoever it was was well and truly trapped. Which was OK, Sophie told herself, unless they turned out to be violent.

Very, very slowly, on tiptoe, trying to avoid the slightest creak of a board under her weight, which would warn of her approach, Sophie made her way towards the first room. Gently, she pushed on the half-closed door.

The door's rusty hinges squeaked slightly in protest as it swung open. But apart from some bits of broken furniture, the room was empty. For protection, Sophie picked up a heavy chair leg from the pile and, as she hefted it, felt a little more confident. But as she moved on to the next room, Sophie knew she was involved in a crazy game of Russian roulette. Each time a room was eliminated, the danger of the next being the intruder's hiding-place was greatly increased.

Sophie slowly worked her way along the row. By the time she'd drawn a blank and only two more closed doors remained, she paused. Which to choose? There had been footprints outside all the doors, but the ones outside the last remaining doors were the clearest of all.

Even without bending down, Sophie easily identified the squirls and geometric patterns made by the treads of trainers. Oliver always wore trainers, and she was convinced he'd been up here before, on at least one occasion.

But so did Carl.

For that matter, so did lots of people. Today, even she was wearing trainers with her white tracksuit.

The only way she would ever find out who the prints belonged to, was by pushing open both doors in turn. Standing well back, in case of attack, Sophie gave the right-hand door a sharp prod with the chair-leg. It swung more easily than the others and, as it opened, Sophie ducked in alarm as a black, flapping shape headed straight for her at high speed.

The rook she'd released swooped low over her head and then flew frantically around the loft, beating its black wings and opening its sharp grey beak wide, in squawks of alarm. In its panic it flew towards the main source of light, where it collided with the grimy window, leaving behind, imprinted in the dust, a blurred outline of its outspread wings.

Covered with grime, and trailing bits of old cob-webs, the rook turned and flew up into the eaves. When its malevolent eye spotted Sophie, the bird dived directly at her head with all the reckless regard for its own life as that of a kamikaze pilot. The revival of her old childhood terror was suddenly doubled, as it was coupled in Sophie's mind with the horrifying probability that this rook's ancestors had once greedily pecked out Seth Garner's eyes.

Fearing the worst and only too aware of her already tingling scalp, Sophie dropped the chair-leg with a clatter. Desperate, she tried to cover her face and head with her hands and arms.

Maybe it was the sudden gesture which frightened the diving bird. Or perhaps it was Sophie's pale blonde hair that enraged it. It could simply have mistaken the glint of the ring on her finger for that of a predator's eye. Either way, the bird went crazy. It flew at Sophie, catching at her with its claws. Then it swirled around her head, squawking and pecking her hands with its long, pointed beak.

Sophie retreated from the beating, black wings, back across the loft towards the stairs, but in her frantic efforts to twist away from the bird, she slipped in some wet bird-droppings and crashed on to the floor. Even then, though she rolled around the floor and tried to beat the bird off with her hands, it still went for her, refusing to be put off.

Sophie was still desperately trying to defend herself, when she saw, her eyes at floor level, the only remaining door slowly opening. There was just time for Sophie, in the half-light, to catch a glimpse of a white trainer before the bird intensified its frenzied attack and she was again forced to shield her eyes.

When she next got the chance to peep between her scratched fingers, all Sophie saw of the intruder was a hand, lowering a trapdoor set in the floor between the drive shaft and the hopper.

'So there *is* another way up here!'

During a brief lull in the bird's vicious attacks, Sophie, on her hands and knees, quickly crawled across the floor until she reached the chair-leg. Grabbing it, this time when the bird dived, Sophie swung the weapon round her head and scared it off just long enough for her to reach and raise the trapdoor.

Beneath it was a perpendicular iron ladder, fastened to the wall, which could easily have been the one beside the foyer entrance. The very ladder Paula had said Oliver was swinging from the night the bricks almost killed her. Though the ladder was still vibrating as whoever it was rapidly shinned down it, Sophie knew they had too long a start on her. The only way she might possibly catch up was by using the staircase.

Still whirling the chair-leg round her head like a helicopter blade, Sophie charged back, and escaped from the rook. But she'd only got one floor down the stairs before she heard the distant bang of the stage door and knew it was too late. Whoever it was, had escaped.

Dirty, hurt and disappointed, Sophie sank down on the stairs. 'Damn! Damn! Damn!'

Then, on the landing beside her, although there wasn't quite so much dust as on the floor above, Sophie noticed a great many more fainter, but identical footprints. But this time they went in and out of the second floor. Surely she'd chased the thief straight up to the top of the building? There hadn't been time for these prints to be made today. So maybe this wasn't the first time the thief had been in the building.

Sophie followed the tracks, which led her down a dingy, narrow corridor and directly to a funny sort of cupboard door, set low in the wall, beneath a short flight of steps. Still trying to recover from her terrifying ordeal with the rook, and dreading what might leap out on her next, Sophie carefully turned the mildewed brass handle and opened the door.

Inside, the limited floor space was almost filled by an unrolled, plain blue sleeping-bag. Beside it lay a couple of dirty mugs, a crumpled Snickers wrapper and two rotting apple cores.

'Well, at least I've found the rat's nest!' said Sophie, pleased that something had come out of her exploits.

But the feeling of triumph quickly faded, as Sophie suddenly realized the blue sleeping-bag looked awfully familiar. Carl had one exactly like it.

Did that mean it was Carl she'd been chasing and

not some anonymous thief? He might easily have been hiding there for weeks, living off their supplies while he watched her every move. No wonder he'd found it so easy to put that horrible note on the board by the stage door.

The idea that without realizing it she'd been so close to Carl, sent Sophie scrambling to her feet and careering recklessly down the stairs.

Ignoring the dark and any possible danger, Sophie fled across the stage. More than once she tripped and was even sent sprawling headlong, but she always hauled herself up and stumbled on. Eventually, she burst out through the stage door where, blinded by the sudden sunlight, she ran straight into Oliver.

Seven

Though Sophie tried to twist out of his grip, Oliver was too strong for her and held on firmly. 'Sophie, what on earth's happened to you?'

'Nothing,' she said, still struggling to escape. 'Nothing at all!' She couldn't ignore the disconcerting coincidence that whenever something unpleasant happened to her, Oliver always seemed to be close at hand.

'But look at you!' he said. 'Your hands are all scratched and bleeding, and you're covered in cobwebs and dirt!'

As Sophie calmed down a little, she glanced at her hands and the patches of grime and bird-dirt, which were smeared all over her once white tracksuit. 'Somebody got into the theatre,' she said. 'You remember all that coffee and stuff which disappeared? Well, it seems somebody's been camping out, for some time, in a little cupboard up on the second floor.'

Sophie could have sworn Oliver looked far more startled by her explanation than he had when she ran into him. His eyes searched hers. 'Did you get a chance to see who it was?'

Why did he sound so uneasy? 'Not really.'

'But you look as if you've been fighting.'

Sophie half laughed. 'All I fought, believe it or not, was a bird! If I hadn't been attacked by this mad rook, I'd have been able to see who the thief was. As it is, all I saw was part of a white trainer,' she pointed at Oliver's feet, 'a bit like yours, and then a hand lowering a trapdoor.'

Oliver noticeably relaxed. 'That's a relief!'

'What do you mean?' Sophie demanded.

He looked decidedly shifty. 'I mean . . . a relief you weren't hurt . . . That's to say, that you weren't hurt any more.'

Sophie was getting confused again. Just when she thought, like it or not, she'd managed to identify the intruder as being Carl, Oliver not only turned up, but was reacting very strangely.

'Oliver, what exactly are you doing here anyway?'

He bent down and gathered together a pile of newspapers, which she'd knocked out of his hands when she cannoned into him. 'I came to make a start on some papier mâché for the masks.'

If Oliver's eyes hadn't avoided hers while he was giving what sounded a perfectly reasonable explanation, she might have believed him. As it was, Sophie no longer knew what to think.

If, as Sophie believed, it was Carl she'd been chasing round the Mill, then why did it matter to Oliver whether she'd seen him or not?

'How did you expect to get into the Mill?' Sophie asked. 'It's always locked up, except for rehearsals.'

Oliver blushed slightly. 'Look, if you must know, I asked Eddie last night and he told me you'd be here.'

'So making the masks was all an excuse?'

'Not really, they've got to be done,' said Oliver, 'but you've been avoiding me these last few days and I thought I might get the chance to find out why.'

Far from making anything clearer, everything Oliver said confused Sophie more, particularly the part about knowing she was going to be there. His excuse that he wanted to talk to her could be just that, an excuse. His real purpose might as easily have been to finish off the job the falling bricks had failed to achieve.

Not wishing to be alone with him, Sophie was about to make her own excuse about having to go home and change, when Paula came bouncing over the bridge.

'Sorry I'm so late,' she called out as she ran towards them, 'but when I got up this morning, I realized if I didn't go to the launderette first I'd be reduced to body-painting!' Paula's mouth suddenly dropped open as she got close enough to take in the state of Sophie. 'What have you been doing, mud-wrestling?'

'It's a long and complicated story,' said Sophie with a relieved grin.

'Oh good,' Paula said. 'Well, I've brought some coffee and milk, so let's go inside while you tell it.'

After Sophie had washed and Paula had made coffee, Sophie barely began her story before Oliver, probably realizing he was neither likely to learn anything new, or get a chance to talk to Sophie alone, took his coffee to the workshop and started on the papier mâché.

By the time Sophie finished, having carefully left out any specific reference to Carl, Paula's coffee stood in front of her, cold and untouched.

'Poor Sophie!' she laid a hand on Sophie's. 'What a terrible thing to happen. I'd have been frightened out of my wits.'

'I was. But more by the bird than the intruder. At least he was running away. The bird kept coming straight for me.'

'We'd better tell Eddie about that woman-eating rook, but I bet he'll be horrified to find out somebody's been living in the building.'

Sophie felt a little guilty about holding back on her suspicions as to the intruder's identity, but it was difficult when she couldn't make up her mind whether the trainer she'd seen belonged to Carl, Oliver, or someone else entirely. 'It seems such an odd place for anyone to choose to hide.'

'Probably just some homeless teenager,' said Paula, 'looking for somewhere warm to kip.'

'But why pick a building that's locked up most of the time? That means, apart from the odd occasion when Eddie's here alone, they would only be able to get in or out in the evening, during rehearsal.'

'Yes, that is a bit odd,' Paula agreed, 'but it explains the missing food and stuff. They must have been starving, locked in here all day!' She delved down into her carrier-bag and pulled out the component parts of the black robe which she would wear as part of the chorus. 'I suppose I'd better get started on this.'

'Did you bring the other dress with you too?'

From a second bag, Paula pulled out several pieces of turquoise material.

'Oh, Paula, with your red hair that'll look fantastic!'

'Mmm. I thought it might turn the odd head too!' Paula said with a satisfied grin. 'To be honest, I chose the material so that, when the show's over, I can cut it down into a nice little evening number. Where's yours?'

Sophie held up, under her chin, the part-finished dress, which was in deep blue.

'Sophie, that's lovely!'

'Yes, it's a pity I only get to wear it for about five minutes,' Sophie said, searching through her bag for matching cotton. 'I spend most of the play wearing that horrible, shapeless white shift.'

'You're quite lucky to be allowed the white shift!' Paula said. 'Nathan keeps on saying, to be authentic you ought to be forced to do the torture scene in the nude.'

'Over my dead body!' Sophie said. 'Oh damn!'

'What's up?

'I must have left my blue cotton at home.'

'I haven't got anything remotely like it, I'm afraid.'

'Never mind,' Sophie said, 'I'll pop into town and get some.'

'Try Mercers down Tythe Street,' Paula suggested. 'It's on the right, at the end of the High Street.'

'Right. I've still got some posters to drop off, so I can do those at the same time. You don't mind if I leave you alone here, after what happened to me?'

'Oh, I'll be all right,' Paula said confidently. 'I should think you've frightened the thief off for good. Anyway, I don't intend to go roaming around the building, not while that bird's still on the loose, and, besides, I've got Oliver here to protect me.'

Although Sophie could no longer think of Oliver's presence as being a plus, it was up to Paula to make her own decision. 'OK, I won't be gone long.'

'Don't you think you ought to change before you go out?' Paula said, pointing to Sophie's grubby tracksuit.

'I'd forgotten! I know, I've got an old pair of jeans and a shirt in the dressing-room. I'll change into those.'

Paula looked concerned. 'Are you sure you'll be all right up there? Want me to come with you?'

Sophie smiled. 'Thanks, I'll be fine. Just come if I scream.'

'Scream early in that case!' Paula laughed. 'I don't want to trip over your mutilated corpse.'

Sophie thought it was odd that Paula, after listening to her story, could still make a remark like that, even as a joke, and wished she could dismiss everything that had happened so easily.

On the way to the dressing-room, Sophie glanced into the workshop. There was a tin bath, half-full of pulped newspaper, but no sign of Oliver.

Mercers turned out to be an old-fashioned shop which not only still stocked thousands of buttons in everything from plastic to silver and held a positive library of knitting patterns, but also had every conceivable colour and type of cotton, arranged in a vast rainbow of shades. It was run by elderly twin sisters, who hovered together around customers the way butterflies cluster round flowers. They also had a confusing tendency to finish each other's sentences.

'Was it pale blue . . .'

'. . . or dark you needed?'

'A deep blue.' Sophie chose a reel. 'I think this one.'

'A lovely colour. Ninety-five . . .'

'. . . pence, please.'

After Sophie had paid for the cotton, she peeled a poster off the roll she was carrying under her arm. 'Could you possibly display a poster for our play somewhere in your shop?'

The two women put their heads close together to read it. 'The Testing of . . .'

'. . . Agnes Wishart.'

'It sounds very . . .'

'. . . exciting. Yes, of course . . .'

'. . . we will.'

'That's very kind of you both.'

'Though we'll have to be very careful . . .'

'. . . where we put it. After what's happened . . .'

'. . . in the Square.'

Not quite sure what they were going on about, Sophie thanked them and left.

Rather more easily, she disposed of another two posters and was about to make her way back to the Mill, when, amongst the busy throng of weekend shoppers, she caught sight of Oliver, who she thought she'd left working at the theatre, walking along on the opposite side of the High Street.

Sophie crossed over, trying to weave her way between people and catch up with him. She was about to call his name, when she realized he wasn't alone. Curious to know why Oliver was always saying one thing, like going to make the papier mâché, and then doing another, she decided to follow him at a distance. At least Oliver was easy to keep track of, being a head taller than most of the people around him.

As he walked along, he was waving a hand in the air, to emphasize the point he was making, and was

71

obviously getting very worked up about what he was saying to the boy walking beside him. Wearing black jeans and T-shirt, the boy was almost as tall as Oliver, but much slimmer, and he had jet-black hair, cropped exceptionally short.

As Sophie drew closer, she thought she heard Oliver shout something like, 'How did you think you could get away with it?'

The boy obviously didn't like the question and tried to move away from Oliver.

As the two stopped, like rocks parting the flow of shoppers, and angrily turned to face each other, Sophie clearly saw two things: one, that Oliver was holding the other person firmly by the wrist, and two, it wasn't a boy he was with, but a girl. And a very attractive girl at that.

It was her close-cropped hair which had misled Sophie and which also gave the girl a very appealing quality, halfway between elf and urchin. The short hair also emphasized the girl's already prominent cheek-bones and enlarged her flashing emerald-green eyes into huge, perfect oval dishes. For somebody who swore he hadn't got a girlfriend and wasn't involved with anyone, Oliver seemed to have a very close relationship with this devastating-looking girl.

To avoid being seen, Sophie slipped into the entrance of a jeweller's. Pretending to examine a display of earrings, she watched through the right angle of the shop window and waited to see what would happen. The girl was still struggling, desperately trying to twist her slender wrist free of Oliver's strong grip.

Though, unfortunately, Sophie was too far away to hear what he was saying, Oliver appeared to be alternating between pleading with the girl and shouting at her, the scar on the side of his face standing out far more prominently than usual. The girl, her long, slim legs firmly braced as she tried to tug herself away, obviously didn't agree with what Oliver was saying. She'd shut her eyes, to keep him out, and was violently shaking her head back and forth.

Passers-by were beginning to notice them too. An old lady, weighed down with shopping, stood right next to them, openly watching their argument. Oliver tugged the girl to him, tried to hold her in his arms, but she wriggled free with such a violent twist she almost knocked over the old lady before darting out into the busy traffic.

Oliver shouted after her, 'Kate! Kate, come back here!' But his voice was lost, as angry drivers hooted at her.

The old lady looked shocked, then laughed. She was obviously enjoying the whole thing more than anything she'd recently seen on the telly.

Oliver tried to follow, but wasn't as lucky as Kate had been. He narrowly avoided being knocked down by a delivery van, which skidded to a sharp halt, surrounded by the smell of burnt rubber. Without bothering to apologize to the driver, Oliver ran after Kate, but paused in mid-flight, to turn quickly, to and fro, looking over heads, but couldn't find her.

Sophie had seen Kate slip away down a side-street, without a single backward glance. Eventually, she watched Oliver stuff his hands deep into the pockets of his jeans before slouching off down the High Street, looking very fed up at losing her.

The drama over, Sophie emerged from her hiding-place wondering what all the fuss had been about and, most important of all, who was Kate? If only because of the way Oliver had manhandled her in public, it seemed obvious they knew each other well.

There were aspects of the scene she'd just witnessed which reminded Sophie, uncomfortably, of her own tempestuous relationship with Carl. How often they'd had similar stand-up rows in shops, with Sophie desperate to run away, and Carl refusing to release her.

So, who was Kate and why had Oliver never mentioned her, not even to Paula? For that matter, why had Oliver and Kate never once been seen together, until now?

Sophie was still trying to find answers to all those questions as she crossed the Square and came face to face with one of Andrew's fly-posters, obviously the one the Mercer sisters had remarked on. It was pasted on the window of an empty shop, amongst a selection of others advertising bankruptcy sales and pop concerts.

As she looked more closely, Sophie's hand covered her mouth to avoid crying out loud from shock.

No longer was the poster solely black and white. To the picture of Agnes, a sick-minded graffiti artist had added a stream of brilliant red blood. It was spurting from a gaping stab wound in her stomach, ran vividly down the white shift, and ended in a large crimson pool at her feet.

The artist's lurid addition of the blood transformed Agnes's pose from a plea for mercy, to one of a body dying in agony.

Sophie, only too aware that the face on the poster was hers, wanted to shut her eyes, to run away; anything to escape from the vicious image. But instead she froze, her eyes continually drawn back to the hideously defaced poster.

When she finally managed to drag her eyes down from the horrific picture, Sophie saw that her name, amongst the list of performers, had been totally obliterated by a thick black line, drawn in the shape of a coffin.

Eight

'Don't take it so seriously,' Paula said, trying to reason with Sophie, who had returned to the Mill in a dreadful state. 'Cranks do that kind of crazy thing all the time. To them, drawing on posters means no more than it does to kids who put moustaches and spectacles on pictures in newspapers.'

'But, Paula, this wasn't innocent fun. It was horrible, as if they really meant it to happen!'

'Oh, I'm sure you're mistaken.'

'Well, if it was only intended as some kind of sick joke,' Sophie asked, 'why go to the trouble of blotting my name out as well, and with a black coffin, of all things?'

'I'm sure the whole thing's probably nothing more than coincidence,' Paula said. 'I've seen posters with swastikas sprayed on them, but I bet half of the people who do it don't even know what they mean. I really think you're adding two and two together to make five.'

'But anybody can see that it's *me* on the poster with the blood pouring out, not Agnes!'

'Hang on!' Paula said. 'Aren't you making rather a lot of that? After all, it's only people in the cast who know that you're even playing Agnes. The cast list on the poster has all our real names in alphabetical order, not the parts we're playing.'

'You surely don't mean that somebody who *doesn't* know me is responsible?'

'I think that's more likely, don't you?'

'But, Paula, so many things have happened to me now,' Sophie insisted. 'The falling bricks . . . '

'Eddie was positive that was an accident,' Paula pointed out.

'But what if it wasn't?'

'Well, that still doesn't mean they were intended for you. We all use this green-room. They could have dropped on any one of us.'

'And then there's the thief who's been living in the building for goodness knows how long. Suppose it was the thief who altered that poster and they've been lurking up there, waiting for a chance to kill me!'

'But why, Sophie? People don't usually just go round killing people for no reason. Even the guy who killed John Lennon had a reason. It never made sense to the rest of us, and it certainly didn't justify what he did, but it made sense to him at the time, and that's the point. Who in the world could possibly have any reason to kill you, Sophie?'

'John Lennon didn't matter to the guy who killed him. Killing Lennon was just a way of getting himself noticed by Jodie Foster, with whom he was obsessed.'

'At least that rules out the possibility of somebody wanting to kill you just to impress someone!' Paula said. 'Not wishing to be rude, but you can hardly claim that you playing Agnes puts you in the same league as John Lennon!'

Sophie sighed. If only she could tell Paula everything she knew. But that would only make sense if she'd mentioned Carl to Paula when they'd first met. To tell her now would probably only sound like more adding two and two to get five.

Sophie decided to take the easy way out. 'I suppose you're right,' she said. 'But what's been done to me on the poster does remind me of what Angie said.'

Paula pulled a face. 'Which particular bit? Angie comes up with so many weird ideas!'

'The bit about me being the thirteenth member of the company. I'm beginning to wish I'd never agreed to be in the play at all.'

'Oh, come on! Everything will be all right, you'll see,' Paula said, and then, to try and cheer Sophie up, added, 'I tell you what, I'm going to a club tonight. Why don't you come with me, see if we can find ourselves a couple of useful guys? At least it would take your mind off all this for a bit.'

Sophie smiled, but shook her head. 'Thanks for the offer, but I've wasted hours and there's still so much work to do on my dress. Apart from that, as there isn't a rehearsal tonight and it's been a pretty rough day, I wouldn't mind getting an early night.'

'Oh well, suit yourself!' Paula began to put away her work.

Sophie looked uneasy. 'Are you going right now?'

'I've had enough for today,' Paula said, 'and anyway, if I'm going to get lucky tonight, I'll need time to give myself the full treatment!'

'In that case, I'll pack up too,' Sophie said. 'I don't

really want to stay here on my own and you can show me where Swan Lane is. I promised Eddie I'd take the key back after we've locked up.'

When Paula, despite Sophie's feeble excuses to try and keep her there, abandoned her at the end of Swan Lane, Sophie comforted herself with the thought that at least it was still daylight.

But as she walked down the street of small, neat, terraced houses, whose front doors opened directly on to the pavement, Sophie realized she'd forgotten the number of Eddie's house. She couldn't remember whether he'd said twenty-eight, or twenty-six. Both sounded right, but having already got on the wrong side of him, dropping the key through the wrong letter-box would be the final straw.

Besides, she wanted to see him, to apologize for the misunderstanding over who'd taken the coffee. Perhaps if she told him about chasing out the intruder, she might get back into his good books again.

She chose number twenty-eight and knocked. There was a good deal of drawing of bolts and barking before an old lady, bent double as she desperately hung on to the collar of an irate and overweight dachshund, opened the door a crack.

'I'm sorry to bother you –' Sophie began.

But the yelping of the dog was making it difficult for the old lady to hear, so she cupped her free hand to her ear. 'What'd you say?'

'I'm looking for Eddie.'

The woman, who was going purple in the face from the effort of coping with the struggling, snapping dog, yelled at Sophie, 'Who d'you want?'

Sophie shouted, 'EDDIE!'

'Oh, you mean Mr Garner! Next door!' she shouted back, inclining her head towards number twenty-six and immediately slamming her own front door before either the dog, or she, collapsed in a fit.

Sophie was astonished to hear that Eddie's surname was Garner. He must have been a relative of the old miller, Seth Garner. No wonder he knew so much about the Mill, and that he'd got upset when he overheard Angie talking about Seth's ghost. She was having second thoughts about bothering to knock, but the door of number twenty-six opened before she'd even reached it and Eddie thrust his head out.

'Oh, it's you, disturbing the whole neighbourhood!' he said. 'I said drop it through the letter-box. There was no need to go waking up half the street!'

'I'm sorry, I forgot your number.'

'Oh, I see. Well, where is it then?'

But Sophie kept the key in her pocket. 'Look, Eddie, I'm sorry about this morning. I didn't mean to suggest you'd taken the stuff. In fact, I think I've found out who did.'

'Oh aye?'

Sophie gave him a shortened version of the story that included both the rook and the intruder.

Eddie looked quite impressed. 'Living in a cupboard up on the second floor, you say? Well, I never! But you didn't get a proper look at him?'

'I'm afraid not,' Sophie said with a shake of her head, thinking it wise not to pass on any guesswork about the identity of the culprit.

'Well, I should think you've frightened him off all right! But I'll have to keep a better look out, to see he doesn't get back in again, and I'll sort that bird out too!' Eddie's attitude was now noticeably friendlier. 'Thanks for taking the trouble to tell me.'

'You're welcome,' she said, handing over the key. 'I hadn't realized, until the lady next door said, that you were related to Seth Garner.' The moment she finished speaking, Sophie felt the temperature drop back several degrees.

'It's not the kind of thing you go round shouting about.' Eddie looked at her with his cold, grey eyes. 'He were my great uncle.'

'But there's nothing to be ashamed of . . .'

Eddie cut in on her sharply. 'I never said there was!'

'I mean,' Sophie persisted, 'if I was descended from Henry the Eighth, or Dick Turpin, I wouldn't mind people knowing.'

'Aye,' Eddie said darkly. 'Well, maybe there's a difference when you know what happened to them. It's all the stupid lies that have built up around Seth, with not knowing, that gets under my skin. Like yon lass, talking about ghosts and suchlike.'

'I can understand how you feel,' Sophie sympathized.

But Eddie wasn't in the mood. 'Oh no you can't! Not unless you've lived through it! I've had people pointing the finger at me all my life, ever since I were a lad at school, and they haven't stopped yet!'

'I'm sorry . . .'

But again Eddie interrupted. 'If you'll excuse me, I'm in the middle of me tea.' And with that, he slammed the door in Sophie's face.

On Sunday morning, Sophie woke to find tears of rain

streaming down her windows as she looked out into the deserted park. For a while she lay still, thinking how much her life had closed in on her during the previous week. It was hard to realize that only a week ago she was thoroughly enjoying everything, had hardly a care and was free to go wherever she liked, without hesitation. Suddenly all that had changed. In the street she was constantly checking to see nobody was following, and the theatre no longer seemed the friendly place it once was.

A week earlier Sophie would have happily leapt at Paula's invitation to go to the disco. Yesterday she'd turned it down with the feeble excuse that she wanted to catch up with her sewing. The real reason was that hideous poster. Since she'd seen it, Sophie no longer felt safe out anywhere. It had been bad enough when she believed only Carl was behind all the mysterious happenings. Then Oliver got tangled up in her list of suspects. That was a bitter blow, no longer being able to trust the person she had come to rely on most.

But what if neither of them had anything to do with the grotesque alterations to the poster? In that case yet another person was harbouring some sort of awful grudge against her and, while she knew what Carl and Oliver looked like, this new enemy was faceless.

But maybe they weren't entirely unknown. It could easily be somebody she was close to every day. Even another member of the company. Marge for instance. She'd always sworn she was perfectly happy for Sophie to take over the role of Agnes from her. But what if, secretly, she bitterly resented Sophie stealing the part away and was so jealous, she was planning to wreak a terrible revenge?

'Oh, come on!' Sophie said out loud. 'Marge is the kindest, most inoffensive person in the whole world. If you suspect her, then you really are paranoid!' She remembered the old joke: 'No, you're not paranoid, everyone really *is* out to get you!' But it no longer brought the slightest trace of a smile to her face.

After everything that had happened, the only place she felt safe was locked inside her own flat. Even there, while she'd been sewing last night, she'd tried to drown out the silence with music from her stereo, only to turn it down every time she heard the slightest creak on the landing outside her door. She must have been over to the window a thousand times, to check that anyone going out had locked the front door properly.

The trouble was, everything had got too complicated. It was all whirling round and round in her head until she no longer knew *what* she believed. She couldn't *prove* the thief was really Carl. Anyone could have put the anonymous letter together, and there must be thousands more sleeping-bags just like the one she'd found.

Nevertheless, deep down, Sophie still felt everything that had happened — the letter, the watcher in the park, the falling bricks and someone hanging around in the theatre, even the disfiguring of the poster — pointed towards the sort of malicious, vindictive behaviour that came as second nature to Carl. But in that case, where did Oliver fit in? And who was Kate? And what had Oliver done to Kate which made her so desperate to escape from his clutches? Kate was obviously frightened of Oliver, which Sophie felt gave her every reason to feel the same way.

Unable to find any answers, and suffocated by the questions which crowded in on her from every side, Sophie admitted defeat. Wrapping the duvet tightly around her, she curled up into a ball in the middle of her bed and stayed that way for the rest of the day. Some of the time she slept, but while she was awake she didn't eat or drink, she simply lay there, trying to blot out the world.

That night, Sophie was being chased by men, on foot and on horseback, across an unfamiliar area of the park. The light of the full moon was frequently hidden by huge, driven clouds. A thin mist hung amongst the trees, hovering a few metres above the damp ground. Owls out hunting hooted before sweeping down, silent as dark shadows, over their prey.

Although Sophie couldn't see her pursuers, she could hear them, even above the rasping noise of her own forced breathing, crashing through the under-growth around her. A sudden stabbing pain caused her to grip her stomach. She thought she must have a stitch, but when she took away her hand, it was sticky with her own blood, which glistened, black, in the moonlight. The pain became sharper, more intense, but still she ran on, tripping and stumbling across the uneven ground.

Then suddenly, in addition to the owls and the pounding hoof beats, there was a new sound. A hoarse, barking roar, which echoed across the parkland and could have been a beast in pain. But Sophie recognized it for what it was: a rutting deer, warning off rival stags.

After Sophie collapsed on to the ground, through

84

the earth she could feel the relentless drumming vibrations from the hooves of her pursuers, as they tightened their deadly cordon around her. Too exhausted to move, she rolled over on to her back, defenceless, and waited in the clearing for her attackers.

When the men first appeared, they halted on the clearing's edge, lurking amongst the dark strength of the tree trunks, their faces concealed beneath dark hoods. One by one, they dismounted from their coal-black steeds, drew their daggers, the blades glinting wickedly in the moonlight, and slowly advanced towards her. Sophie lay still, watching and waiting for them to strike. There was nothing else she could do.

But, when they were only halfway across the clearing, they suddenly halted and appeared uncertain. Their horses tossed their manes, showed the whites of their bloodshot eyes and whinnied. A huge shadow, cast by the moon, fell across Sophie's prostrate body. Cloven hooves pawed the ground either side of her head and her nostrils were filled by the warm, musky tang of deer.

Glancing upwards, she saw, silhouetted against the moonlight, the magnificent head of a stag, its huge antlers branching out into points that were turned silver by the beams. The stag eyed the men angrily, then threw back its mighty head and let out an enormous, threatening roar which echoed through the wood.

When Sophie turned back, the men and horses had melted away into the shadows and the wood was once more silent.

Struggling to her feet, Sophie said to the stag, 'Thank you for rescuing me.' But as she reached out to pat its nose affectionately, the stag snorted and rose up on its hind legs, menacingly high above her, its front hooves thrashing the air.

It was only then that Sophie realized her ordeal was far from over. The huge, traitorous stag had driven off the men purely for his own purposes.

As she backed away, the stag dropped his head so that the bristling antlers pointed directly at her and charged. Sophie screamed, and seconds later she felt the searing pain as the strong, multipointed antlers pierced through her flesh in several places, simultaneously.

Sophie woke, sweating and trembling, fighting off the duvet as she thrashed around, before subsiding into a lonely stillness.

Eventually, feeling the cold night air on her skin, Sophie pulled her towelling robe around her and wandered across the room. Rain was still drumming on the windows.

Sophie pressed her feverish forehead against the ice-cold glass and gazed fearfully out into the darkness. The rain-streaked pane distorted her view of the park and it no longer seemed the friendly place it had once been.

Nine

Frightened to sleep, for fear of what became a recurring nightmare, and worn out as a result, Sophie was enormously relieved to watch a watery dawn break on Monday morning. She had spent the whole night huddled in her duvet, sitting at the head of her bed, knees drawn up under her chin and her back thrust into the angle of the wall.

Her legs felt shaky as she climbed stiffly out of bed. There was a nasty taste in her mouth and a slightly sick, burning sensation in the pit of her stomach. But when she glanced in the mirror, Sophie was horrified by the reddened, haunted eyes which stared back at her. There were also dull, grey patches beneath both eyes and they were framed by hair which hung in tangled clumps, like lifeless blonde string.

Her first inclination was to forget all thoughts of going to the office – simply to ring in and say she was sick. But then she had a sudden change of heart.

'This can't go on! If you spend another day alone in this flat you really will go mad!' she told her reflection. 'You can't hide away for ever. What you need is company.'

Several times during Sunday, Sophie had considered ringing Paula and inviting her round. The fact that she didn't was yet another result of not knowing who to trust. But the office was different. It would be imposs- ible for anyone to harm her surrounded by other people.

'You've got to get a grip on yourself and fight back before it's too late.' This sounded fine in theory, until Sophie wondered how she was supposed to fight an anonymous enemy, someone who had succeeded in worming their way into every corner of her life, whether awake or asleep.

'But it's got to be now or never!'

Feeling slightly better after a shower and a cup of strong coffee, but still unable to face the thought of food, Sophie made her way through the pouring rain to the office.

Paula, who could hardly fail to notice how dreadful Sophie looked, tactfully inquired, 'Are you OK?'

'Yes, I'm fine,' Sophie lied. 'I think I might be getting a cold.'

'I rang Nathan yesterday and told him about you finding somebody roaming around the Mill.'

'Did you mention the poster?'

Paula nodded. 'Yes, that too. He said you shouldn't worry about it. He thinks, like I do, that it isn't really directed at you personally and it was probably just a sick joke, done by somebody with a rather ghoulish sense of humour.'

In spite of finding it difficult to get her befuddled mind to concentrate on her work, Sophie felt much more comfortable with the buzz of the busy office around her. So much so that, at lunchtime, she ate for the first time in twenty-four hours: a granary roll filled with cottage cheese. But she was very grateful when Paula suggested they walk together to rehearsal.

When they arrived they could hardly get through the stage door for Nathan. He had his back to them and was hemmed in by most of the rest of the cast. Over the weekend they had suddenly been struck by the obvious truth: having enjoyed the luxury of months of rehearsal, there was only one week left.

'We open on Saturday!' Pete was saying. There was an anxious look on his thin face and more than a hint of nerves in his voice.

Nathan was unmoved. 'That's exactly what I've been telling you all for days.'

'But half the costumes aren't finished,' Marge said, 'and apart from Tim's frames, the masks are barely started.'

Tim spoke up. 'I've got two more rostra to paint yet, and if you insist on using them for rehearsal I'll never get them done.'

Nathan nodded. 'Yes, I know all about that too.'

'And we still haven't done anything about the final act,' said Angie. 'We'll *never* be ready to open in time.'

'Look!' Nathan held his hands up for quiet. 'I know you're all getting nervous, but really, there's nothing to worry about!' A babble of voices instantly broke out and Nathan had to raise his voice to make himself heard. 'Listen! Apart from tonight, we've got three more days before the first dress rehearsal on Friday. Which means five days to opening night, including all day Saturday for a second dress rehearsal, when we can iron out any little difficulties that crop up. If we stick at it, we'll be ready, no problem.'

'But there is a great deal to do,' Paula said, 'apart from just the acting.'

'Well, for one thing,' Nathan said calmly, 'my half-term holiday has started. I can come here during the day and get some extra jobs done, like help with the masks. Also, if I came in early one morning I could paint the rostra. That way they'll be dry by the evening, which means we'll be able to keep using them for rehearsals.'

'That would be a help,' Tim admitted.

'Right, now the best thing is, rather than panicking,' Nathan suggested, 'you should all make out lists of everything you know of that still needs doing. Don't put anything on there that you know you can take care of yourself, just the rest. Then, at coffee break, we'll compare notes and sort out who can do what. Organization and hard work are what we need. So let's make a start now, by getting the stage set up for the opening scene.'

The others, soothed by the way Nathan had taken charge, went on into the theatre, leaving Sophie and Paula alone with Nathan.

Nathan turned and looked over his glasses at Sophie. 'Paula told me all about Saturday. I gather you've already had a word with Eddie and I've asked him to have another check on the building's security.'

Nathan sounding so matter-of-fact made Sophie feel a little foolish. 'Thanks.'

'I've also got Andrew to replace the poster in the Square. Let's hope whoever did it leaves that one alone.'

'I hope so too,' Sophie said. 'It really scared me.'

'Don't let it. It's probably only some kids messing about.'

As they moved towards the auditorium Paula held back. 'You go on through, Sophie. I just want to have a quick word with Nathan about my dress.'

After Sophie had gone, Paula turned to Nathan. 'Sorry, that was an excuse to get rid of Sophie. I know you think she's making a lot of fuss about nothing, and I agree, but the trouble is, it's really starting to get to her. She's always been a bit nervous about being in the play, but this has pushed her over the edge.'

'I see,' Nathan said thoughtfully.

'At work today, she was going round looking dreadful, and on Saturday, after she saw the poster, she was talking about dropping out of the play altogether. Nathan, I'm only telling you this so you won't push her too hard tonight.'

'Well, thanks,' he said, but he looked very concerned. 'The trouble is, Sophie's on stage almost throughout the play and although she doesn't have to *do* very much, everything revolves around Agnes. If she isn't going to be up to it . . .'

'Oh, she'll probably be all right, once she's recovered from the weekend.'

'Maybe I ought to have a quiet word with Marge.'

'Why?'

'Just to cover ourselves,' Nathan said. 'After all, Agnes was her part originally, so she knows most of the moves.'

'But you won't take the part away from Sophie, will you?' Paula looked alarmed. 'The way she's behaving at the moment, I think that would be the worst thing that could happen to her.'

'I agree, and I won't do anything yet, but we've got to be prepared for the worst,' Nathan said, 'if only for the sake of the others. After all the months of hard work, I owe it to them to have an understudy ready. It'd be very unfair if we had to cancel because Sophie walks out at the last minute. But for now, I'll just get Marge to watch more closely.'

'But didn't you cancel the order for Marge's blonde wig?'

'You're right, I did!' Nathan sounded glum, but after a deep sigh, he pulled himself together. 'Well, I'll just have to uncancel it, won't I? Come on, let's get going. I want to try and work through the whole play tonight.'

But it turned out to be one of those evenings when, if any little thing could go wrong, it did.

Nathan had just called out, 'Opening positions everyone! Let's take it from the top,' when several people pointed out that Oliver was missing.

Fortunately he burst through the doors at that moment and Nathan yelled, 'Come on, Oliver, we're all waiting for you!'

Oliver, looking very wet but at the same time hot and bothered, got ready for his entrance. 'Sorry, everyone! Got held up.'

Sophie wondered if she was the only one to notice a long, very recently healed scratch down the right-hand side of his face. The kind that could be caused by a fingernail. Another fight with Kate perhaps?

'Cut yourself shaving?' she asked casually.

Oliver coloured slightly. 'Something like that.'

But it seemed that everything was conspiring against them, and Pete, as the Narrator, had barely got through his short opening speech before the next hitch.

NARRATOR: By the time Mathew Hopkins, the witch-hunter, arrived, the town was already agog with anticipation. On a well-remembered, previous visit by Hopkins, no less than thirty women had been taken into the Town Hall, where they were stripped and had pins thrust into their bodies. By this means, most were found guilty of witchcraft, and Hopkins was paid twenty shillings for every convicted woman before they were taken into the square and publicly burned. Being market day, the town was packed when the crier appeared on the steps.

CRIER: [Rings handbell loudly] Oyez! Oyez! By order of the magistrate. Anyone wishing to lodge a complaint of witchcraft against a woman, should bring it before the said magistrate forthwith. Oyez! Oyez!

But as Andrew, who played the minor part of the Crier, rang his bell for a second time, the clapper flew out and hit Angie, one of the chorus of townsfolk, on the toe.

'Ouch!' cried Angie, hopping around on one foot.

'Sorry!' Andrew said, 'I think I've dropped a clanger!'

Everyone burst out laughing. Everyone except Nathan, who was sitting halfway back in the auditorium, making notes. He roared at them, 'Concentrate for goodness' sake! Accidents like that could happen during the performance too, so you'd better get used to dealing with them now. You can't all fall around the stage giggling if the same sort of thing happens on Saturday night.'

'I'm sorry about the bell,' Tim said, with his stage-manager's hat on. 'I'll fix it.'

'Yes, do that!' Nathan snapped. 'Now, let's get on!' Pete moved back into position and continued.

NARRATOR: On this particular day, only one man
             presented himself before the magis-
             trate to lay a complaint: Joshua Read,
             a man of much property in this district,
             but who gained little pleasure from his
             wealth, being a well-known miser. He
             spoke out in open court.

But the play ground to a halt again when Joshua, played by Tim, failed to appear.

'Where the hell's Tim gone?' Nathan shouted from the stalls. 'Will you all please stand by for your entrances! I'm trying to get some flow into it, but we're getting nowhere fast like this!'

Tim stumbled back on stage. 'Sorry, Nathan, I'd gone to fix the bell.'

'Not when you're needed on stage! Get on, it's your line.'

JOSHUA: I wish to complain against Agnes
            Wishart.
NARRATOR: The Magistrate, who knew Agnes well
            from a little girl, was amazed but, for

	fear of accusations that he was siding with the Devil, knew he must perform his duty.
MAGISTRATE:	What is the nature of your complaint?
JOSHUA:	On more than one occasion, I have seen this witch on the borders of my property, accompanied by her black cat.
NARRATOR:	Black cats were commonly regarded as being witches' familiars, and it is a source of mystery that any black cats have survived to the present day. Many old ladies, living alone, who had a black cat and a besom, or broom, found out to their cost it would have been better to have drowned the cat and left the house unbrushed rather than risk losing their lives for harbouring these simple items which were widely suspected as being symbols of witchcraft.
MAGISTRATE:	Mr Read, do you have any other information you wish to lay before the court to substantiate your charge?
JOSHUA:	Indeed I do!
MAGISTRATE:	Then make haste about it!
JOSHUA:	In the same place, on several occasions, I witnessed Agnes Wishart light a fire and prepare, in a pot, a broth of toad's entrails, cow dung, hare's liver

and rags. This noisome brew she left in the field for my cows to drink. Two days later, four of my herd died in terrible pain. Two more died in agony the following day and one more since. All bloated, they were, with blackened tongues. I hold Agnes Wishart responsible and accuse her of performing witchcraft.

MAGISTRATE: Then I have no alternative. Let Agnes Wishart immediately be brought before this court.

'OK, hold it right there!' Nathan called out as he bounded towards the stage. 'Now, we're going to start again, and this time I want a bit of life put into it! And I don't want to see the chorus looking bored and having whispered private conversations with their next-door neighbours. You're supposed to *react* to what's going on, not stand there like cabbages. Let's take it from the top again.'

After that, for a while, everything went better, until they reached the torture scene. Oliver had completed his successful testing of Agnes with his needle, and Pete started his speech.

NARRATOR: They can find no mark because there is none. Nor could there be, for the needle witch-prickers used was as false as is my dagger.
[*The Narrator walks across to Agnes*

*and, gripping the handle of a dagger in
both hands, raises it high above her . . .]*

As Pete raised the dagger, Sophie let out the most
horrendous scream, leapt away from him and then
burst into tears. Everyone quickly gathered round her.

Pete, thinking he was responsible, was particularly
concerned. 'Whatever's the matter? What did I do
wrong?'

'Nothing,' Sophie sobbed, 'it's not you. It's the
poster I saw in the Square on Saturday.'

For the benefit of those who hadn't seen it, Paula
explained. 'Somebody's painted blood on it, spurting
from Agnes's stomach.'

'I covered it up yesterday,' Andrew said quietly.

Sophie blew her nose. 'But when Pete raised that
dagger above me, it brought the whole hideous image
back!'

'Poor Sophie!'

'I know I'm being silly,' Sophie said quietly, 'but
does he have to show how the trick dagger works on
me?'

Nathan scratched his head for a moment, while he
looked at the script. 'Well, it's more effective that way,
but I suppose, no, he doesn't *have* to. Let's see, Pete,
there are several members of the chorus around you.
How would it be if you tried out on one of them?'

'Fine by me,' Pete agreed.

'Who's nearest?'

Marge put a hand up. 'I am.'

'OK then, try it on Marge, but because you're side
by side, I think you'll have to stick it in her ribs rather
than her stomach. Get into position and try it.'

Pete obligingly stuck Marge in the ribs with the dagger, and Nathan nodded. 'Yes, that's fine. In fact, being closer to the audience when you do it could have more shock-value.' Nathan turned back to Sophie and slipped his arm round her shoulder. 'But, Sophie, you must try to forget about the poster. After all, whoever did it doesn't know it's really you!'

'It almost certainly isn't just Sophie they're getting at,' said Angie emphatically.

Sophie was puzzled. 'How can you be so sure?'

'Because today I passed at least twelve other posters, either on hoardings or stuck on to shop windows,' Angie replied, 'and every single one had splodges of black paint on it. So it's definitely not just you they've got it in for, Sophie, it's all of us!'

'Oh, lighten up, Angie!' Paula laughed.

But Angie wasn't going to be put off. 'I told you no good would come from having thirteen in the company and interfering with witchcraft!' She paused for effect, and though some smirked behind their hands, their smiles disappeared when she added darkly, 'I think we're all jinxed!'

Ten

'Ten minutes, everybody!' Tim called through the Tannoy.

'How do I look?' Paula asked, as she stood in the centre of the cramped dressing-room which she shared with Sophie and Angie. She performed a twirl, so that the full skirt of her turquoise dress flared outwards.

Sophie, who was peering into the mirror, struggling to pile her hair up under a white cap, turned to admire Paula. 'Wonderful,' Sophie smiled. 'The white ruff sets the whole thing off perfectly.'

'It's all right for you two,' Angie grumbled, 'but I spend all my time wearing this black robe and it makes me look a right pudding!'

Friday's dress rehearsal was about to begin and, much to everyone's amazement, almost everything was ready. Everybody had put in hours of extra work. Not least Andrew, who'd spent every spare minute of the entire week constantly replacing disfigured posters. 'Somebody must have a real grudge against us,' he complained. 'It's almost as if they're following me round doing it! Which I could understand, if it wasn't pouring with rain all the time.'

One rostrum was still a bit tacky and the skull masks were all a trifle damp and smelly from the combination of papier mâché and their coat of luminous yellow paint, but bearing in mind what they had accomplished, that was nothing. The only thing which remained unfinished was the play itself. Despite repeated pleas, Nathan had steadfastly refused to discuss the last two pages of the final act.

As far as Sophie was concerned, the main thing had been that the week had passed without any more nasty shocks or unpleasant surprises. Though still cautious, because there had been no actual signs of the mysterious intruder, she'd gone more into a state of limbo.

She was still suffering nightly repeats of her nightmare of being chased through the park but, although she woke from them trembling, she recovered more quickly from them. She'd kept her distance from Oliver, but he hardly seemed to notice, and Sophie assumed he was preoccupied with thoughts, either of the play, or Kate.

Like the other members of the cast, Sophie was so busy getting ready for the opening night she had forgotten Angie's prediction of impending doom for them all. As she added the final touches to her make-up and then dabbed it off with powder, Sophie found for the first time in weeks she was whistling.

But Angie was horrified. 'Sophie, stop that! Don't you know? You should never whistle in a dressing-room!'

Sophie was mystified. 'Why ever not?'

'It's terribly unlucky. Like quoting from the Unmentionable.'

'The what?'

'Shakespeare's Scottish play,' Angie explained.

'Oh, you mean *Macb* . . .'

Angie screamed to prevent Sophie finishing the word. 'Don't say the title! That's unlucky too.'

Sophie laughed. 'Oh, Angie, that's superstitious nonsense.'

'And I suppose you think it's silly of me to bring Arnold with me?'

It was Paula's turn to look surprised. 'Who's Arnold and where is he hiding?'

'This is Arnold,' Angie said, pointing to a slightly threadbare pink rabbit which hung, suspended by its pink ribbon, between the lights round Angie's dressing-table mirror. She lovingly stroked his tummy. 'I'd never appear in a play unless Arnold was with me.'

'I suppose it's only like touching wood for luck, or not walking under ladders,' Paula agreed.

'I don't care what you say,' Sophie scoffed, 'I just don't believe in any of that stuff.'

But Angie stuck to her beliefs. 'You're entitled to your opinion, but while we're sharing a dressing-room, we all have to respect each other's feelings, and if I believe you've brought bad luck on us by whistling, then you must undo it.'

Sophie struggled to keep her face straight. 'And how do I do that?'

'You have to go outside, turn round three times, swear, then knock and wait to be invited back in.'

Sophie couldn't believe her ears. 'Oh, come on, I've never heard such rubbish!'

'Just do it!' Angie said.

'Oh, go on, Sophie,' Paula urged. 'You might as

well. After all, it makes no difference to you, but at least it'll keep Angie happy.'

'What point is there,' Angie demanded, 'in tempting the fates, when you don't have to?'

'All right, I give in!' Sophie sighed, and, in spite of feeling rather foolish, she left the room and closed the door behind her.

But the moment she was in the dimly-lit corridor, Sophie couldn't help wondering what difference it would make if she simply wandered off? Or if she ignored Angie's ludicrous ceremony and merely knocked on the door to return. Apart from Sophie herself, who'd know?

In the end, she gave in. After all, even though she didn't believe in such things, with everything that had happened, it wouldn't do any harm to avoid tempting the fates any further.

Making sure there was nobody around, Sophie twirled round three times, as instructed, and swore. 'Damn!'

But as she was about to knock on the door, a hand dropped on her shoulder.

'Don't do . . . ' The words died, as Sophie swung round and found herself staring into the eye-sockets of a luminous skull.

Quickly recovering, Sophie exploded. 'I wish you wouldn't be so stupid! That really frightened me.'

But whoever was concealed by the hooded cloak and mask merely waved their arms around and made silly ghost noises. 'Woooo! WOOOO!'

'I don't know who you are, but I don't think it's at all funny!' Sophie snapped.

The apparition completely ignored her and floated off down the corridor.

Sophie banged hard on the dressing-room door and

was inside almost before Angie had a chance to say, 'Enter.'

'Would you believe it?' Sophie stormed. 'Some lunatic just frightened the life out of me by creeping up behind me wearing a skull mask.'

'Who was it?' asked Paula.

Sophie shook her head. 'Who knows! They didn't speak, and behind all the stuff you can't tell who anyone is.'

The Tannoy interrupted. 'Five minutes everybody. Five minutes. Beginners on stage, please.'

Paula took a deep breath. 'Oh well, here we go! Come on, Sophie, you'll be safe with me.'

For a first dress rehearsal, everything went relatively smoothly. Eddie, who'd agreed to operate the lighting controls, missed one or two cues. The odd prop was mislaid and several people forgot their lines, but nothing really awful happened.

During the first interval the cast gathered in the green-room and Nathan said, 'Very few notes, which I'll give to the people concerned later, but the main thing is to start enjoying it! I know it's the first time you've done it in full costume, but you're all a bit wooden. The girls have got to keep their physical posture, but that doesn't mean we have to lose the emotion. OK, any problems?'

Paula held the torn hem of her dress up. 'Did you know there was a length of thick wire sticking out of the steps? I've ripped my dress on it.'

Julian nodded. 'Yes, I caught my ankle on that.'

Nathan turned to Tim. 'Can you sort that?'

'No problem,' Tim said, adding it to his list of 'Things to make and do'.

'I'll go and do it now,' Eddie volunteered. 'I've got a big pair of bolt-cutters. They'll soon cut that off.'

Nathan clapped his hands. 'OK, everybody, finish your coffee and get ready for the second act. And remember, *enjoy!*'

But when Sophie went out on to the stage after changing into her white shift ready for the torture scene, everyone was standing round watching Eddie, who was attacking the offending piece of thick wire with a hacksaw. It made a noise like a nail scraping across glass, and several people, their teeth set on edge, covered their ears.

It was getting late and Nathan was impatient. 'I thought you said you'd got bolt-cutters?'

'I had,' Eddie said, without looking up from his sawing, 'but when I went to look for them, they'd gone from my tool box. You haven't borrowed them, have you Tim?'

'No, I didn't even know you had any,' Tim replied.

'Aye, well, someone has!'

'Look,' Nathan said, 'we must get on.'

Eddie didn't stop hacking away at the wire. 'Hold your horses! I can't leave it sticking out like this. You don't want any more accidents. This'll only take a second now.' And true to his word, Eddie finally cut through the wire.

'All right,' Nathan said, as he headed out into the stalls, 'places for the torture scene.'

Eddie ambled up the aisle. 'You'll have to let me set up me lights first.'

'Yes, quick as you can. And remember, everybody, this time I want some *real* feeling!'

They had hardly started the scene, when Nathan got more than he was expecting. Pete had produced his trick dagger and, forgetting the move had been changed, walked towards Sophie.

From the darkness of the stalls, Nathan boomed. 'You don't do that to Agnes any more. It's Marge, remember?'

'Sorry!' Pete called back, and did the lines again.

NARRATOR: They can find no mark because there is none. Nor could there be, for the needle witch-prickers used was as false as is my dagger.

[*The Narrator walks across to Marge and, gripping the handle of a dagger plunges it, viciously, into her ribs. Marge does not move or make any sound*]

NARRATOR: And the reason she shows no mark, nor makes any sound, is because the dagger is a trick one. The same kind children still use for their games.

[*The Narrator demonstrates by putting his fingertip to the point of the blade and pushing, until the whole blade disappears into the handle*]

But this time when Pete tried to push in the dagger's blade by its point, it did not give. He stared, transfixed by the droplet of his own blood, which had bubbled up on the end of his finger. As if in a dream, Pete realized the blade was stained with far more blood than could have come from his finger. Then, as he turned back to Marge, she slumped to the stage.

Eleven

As the sound of the ambulance's two-tone horn faded into the distance, Nathan took centre stage, his back to the bloodstained patch on the floor, and addressed the cast. 'The ambulanceman said Marge was going to be all right. She'd lost a lot of blood, but they'll soon take care of her and Julian's with her. I thought you ought to know, the last thing Marge said to me before she left was the show has to go on.'

'We can't rehearse without them,' Oliver pointed out.

'No, we can't,' Nathan agreed, 'and I wasn't going to suggest it. I'm sure we won't be getting Marge back in time for the performance. I'll sort out what to do with her part overnight. We'll probably have to redistribute what she does amongst the rest of the chorus. Anyway, it's getting late and we've all had a very distressing experience. I suggest we call it a night and meet back here tomorrow for the second dress rehearsal at midday.'

'You said it was going be a two-thirty start,' said Paula. 'I've got a hair appointment at twelve-fifteen.'

'Yes, I'm sorry, Paula, but none of this was planned, was it? And we've still got a lot to sort out.'

'Including the final act,' Angie said.

For a second, everyone thought Nathan was about to self-destruct, but silently he counted up to ten, before he said, 'Thanks for reminding me, Angie, but I hadn't forgotten. OK, that's it, everybody, but please be on time tomorrow.'

As they walked away together, Andrew said, 'Well, Angie, there's at least one good thing to be said for tonight.'

She looked sideways at him. 'Oh, and what's that?'

'We haven't got a cast of thirteen any more, have we?' he smiled. 'So perhaps the jinx is over!'

Angie wasn't amused. 'Andrew, you're sick, do you know that?' she said, and stalked off.

Several others followed her, and Pete, who'd been very silent since the stabbing and looked grey, even under his stage make-up, walked over to Nathan and said, 'I'm really sorry about this. I should have checked the dagger myself.'

Nathan clapped him on the back. 'Come on, Pete. You mustn't blame yourself. It was a complete accident, Marge said so herself. I wanted to call the police, but she insisted I shouldn't. Go home and get some rest.'

After Pete left, Nathan slumped down on a rostrum. Only Sophie, Paula, Oliver and Tim remained, all sitting gloomily in the semidarkness of the working-light.

'Poor old Pete,' Tim sighed, 'it's me who's supposed to check the props, not him. I'm the one who's responsible for the dagger.'

'But who could have tampered with it and when,

107

that's what I want to know?' Nathan said thoughtfully. 'They not only found time to take it apart and jam the spring, so it wouldn't withdraw, but they'd sharpened the blade until it was like a razor.'

Sophie cleared her throat and spoke very softly. 'If it's anybody's fault,' she said, 'it's mine.' They all looked at her in astonishment. 'I'm the one who brought Carl here.'

Nathan voiced all their thoughts. 'Who the hell is Carl?'

Sophie took a deep breath. 'Carl was an old boy-friend of mine, from my home town. I thought I was in love with him once, until he started to have terrible jealous rages. Then he began to beat me up.'

'You poor thing,' said Paula.

'I stuck it for a while, hoping things would get better, but they didn't and I decided I couldn't put up with it any longer. So I ran away from him and came here, hoping to start a new life.'

Paula squatted down beside Sophie and slipped an arm round her waist. 'Why didn't you tell me any of this before?'

'Because I hoped it was all in the past and, besides,' Sophie continued, 'I was having such a great time and you were all so kind. But now Carl must have caught up with me again!'

'You've seen him around?' Oliver asked.

'Not exactly. First he sent me a note, saying he was watching me, and I'm sure he's been following me everywhere. I'm sure he's the one who's been living here, the one I nearly caught on Saturday, and I'm absolutely positive it was Carl who pushed those bricks down the stairs on top of me.'

'But have you ever once actually seen him here, or anywhere in town?' Oliver insisted.

'No, but they're exactly all the sneaky kind of things he does when he wants to get back at people. Especially this terrible business with the dagger. Only someone as awful as Carl could do a thing like that!'

Nathan looked confused. 'But why would he want to harm Marge, of all people?'

'He didn't, don't you see?' Sophie said. 'That dagger was intended for me!'

Paula frowned. 'Sophie, that doesn't make sense!'

'Yes, it does,' said Sophie. 'We've no idea how long Carl was living here, but I'm sure he was watching my every move until I chased him out last Saturday. Up to that time, Pete used to stick the dagger into *me*. Remember the graffiti on the poster, with all the blood coming out of my stomach? That was Carl telling me how he was going to kill me, but after I saw the poster I asked you if the move could be changed. Now poor Marge is in hospital, and it's all my fault!'

Nathan was very firm. 'Sophie, you really can't hold yourself responsible for what somebody else does.'

'But if I hadn't been in the play,' said Sophie, 'none of this would have happened! All I've done, as Angie is forever pointing out, is brought you all bad luck. I really think I should leave.'

Nathan was horrified. 'You can't do that. With Marge gone I haven't even got an understudy.'

'Anyone could do what I do.'

'But not,' Nathan said firmly, 'as well as you do it, and anyway, to put it bluntly, Sophie, between now and tomorrow night I've got enough problems without you walking out on us.'

Sophie wasn't convinced. 'And suppose I stay and something worse happens?'

Nathan laughed wryly. 'Apart from the end of the world, I can't think of anything worse at the moment. Look, Sophie, I need you and the play needs you, but that apart, if what you say about this Carl character is true, you'll be much safer if we all stick together.'

Sophie was touched. 'Thanks, Nathan.'

'But maybe,' Paula said thoughtfully, 'we really ought to get the police in after all.'

'And tell them what?' Oliver suddenly asked. 'We've no idea who's responsible. I know Sophie thinks it's Carl, but, to be honest, that's all guesswork and there isn't a shred of real proof.'

'Except the things Sophie mentioned have actually happened and somebody definitely *did* tamper with the dagger,' Paula pointed out.

'True,' Oliver agreed, 'but what could they do?'

Paula suggested, 'Offer us a little protection?'

'I suspect,' Oliver said, 'the first thing they'd suggest is cancelling the show. All that business with the posters has already caused a good deal of gossip around town, and if we told the police something really *is* going on, they'd probably make us call off the play, just to be on the safe side.'

Nathan nodded. 'I think Oliver's right. If we're ever to get this play on, we'll just have to be extra vigilant ourselves.'

Eddie interrupted their conversation by shouting across the auditorium, 'I've got a home to go to even if you lot haven't! Come on, I'm waiting to lock up!'

Nathan stood up. 'Sorry, Eddie!'

'Oh, and if you haven't got enough troubles,' Eddie added, 'the roof's sprung a leak.'

'Well, you know what they say,' Paula said with a smile, 'it never rains but it pours.'

But Eddie didn't find the situation remotely amusing. 'Yes, well, it's doing that all right. I've put some buckets underneath the worst leaks, but I'll need to get up there first thing, or you'll have it flowing down the stairs.'

'OK, thanks, Eddie,' Nathan said wearily. He didn't really need any more problems. 'I think I'll pop down to the hospital and see how Marge is.'

Oliver put a hand on Sophie's arm. 'Would you like me to see you home?'

In spite of everything she'd told them, Sophie still couldn't work out where Kate and Oliver fitted into the jigsaw. She'd certainly noticed how quickly Oliver had jumped in the moment Paula suggested getting the police involved. She still thought, until everything was sorted out, it would be better to stay clear of him. 'Thanks, Oliver, but I still feel responsible for what happened to Marge, and so I think I ought go to the hospital with Nathan, if that's all right with you, Nathan?'

'Sure,' said Nathan.

Oliver nodded. 'Good idea, I'll come along too.'

'Sorry,' Nathan said, 'mine's a sports car, so I've only got two seats and, nothing against you, Ollie, but I'd rather have this young lady where I can keep an eye on her. It'll also give me an opportunity to discuss with her an idea I've had for the final act.'

The rain was drumming on the soft top of Nathan's sports car and they were heading for the bridge, when the headlights swept across the swirling, sandy water of the swollen river.

The sight took Sophie by surprise. 'I hadn't realized it had risen so much.'

'Well, it's been raining solidly for a week, and the water off the hills is coming down here now,' Nathan said gloomily. 'I just hope we can get the play over and done with before the Mill ends up flooded.'

'We could ask Tim to knock us up an ark, just in case,' Sophie suggested.

In spite of his deflated state, Nathan managed a half-smile. 'Yes, he'd really love me for that!'

Although by the time Nathan and Sophie arrived at the hospital it was nearly midnight, the accident department was still busy, mainly with repairing Friday night drunks and the fall-out from domestic arguments.

On learning they were both sober and neither of them needed putting back in one piece, the overworked receptionist was very helpful. 'Your friend is still with the doctor. If you'd like to take a seat, I'll call you the minute you can see her.'

Nathan, heading for a quieter corner, paused beside a vending-machine. 'Fancy a coffee or anything? Are you hungry?'

'A hot chocolate, please.'

Nathan slipped coins into the machine and pressed the appropriate buttons. 'Sophie, are you sure you're not hungry?' he asked, adding with a gentle smile, 'We must keep up your strength for tomorrow!'

'It's very kind of you, Nathan, but I think, what with everything that's happened this evening, plus what's ahead of us for tomorrow, if I ate anything, I'd instantly throw up.'

'All that stuff about your ex-boyfriend,' Nathan said, as he skilfully negotiated his way round a couple of lurching drunks without spilling anything from the two plastic cups or dropping the script he had tucked under his arm. 'You don't really know that he's responsible for fixing the dagger, or anything else. I mean, for a start, how would he find you? Who else knows you came here?'

'Only my parents,' Sophie admitted.

'And are they likely to have told him?'

'I doubt it. They hated Carl from the first moment they set eyes on him, and last time I spoke to them they said they hadn't seen Carl for ages. But they're coming over to watch the play tomorrow. I'll ask them again. Now,' Sophie said, anxious to change the subject, 'I thought you wanted to talk about how to end the play?'

'Ah, yes. I think we do need to bring the story as up to date as possible, and Pete can do that in an Epilogue which I've written out here.'

Sophie looked at the handwritten page of script. 'Will there be time for him to learn all that?'

Nathan shook his head. 'No need. He can read it from a book, a bit like Saint Peter waiting at the Pearly Gates. But the main thing is, I want you to be part of it, so the character of Agnes doesn't get lost. I also want to take advantage of all the theatre's entrances and exits, with the chorus, in their black robes and skull masks, carrying lanterns, weaving their way through the audience. That way we get the feeling of being surrounded by the spirits of all the people who were put to death for being witches.'

'Sounds good to me. What will I need to do?'

'As far as you're concerned, it's really a question of floating past Pete towards one exit and then belting round the backstage corridor like a bat out of hell to come in again on the opposite side.'

'Sounds complicated.'

'Not really. Just a matter of choreography and timing more than anything,' Nathan said. 'I thought we could plot everyone's moves at the end of the dress rehearsal so they stay fresh in people's minds for the performance. After your burning scene there should be time for you to clean off your make-up, so you'll look very pale and ghostly. I suppose, to fit in with the others, you ought to be wearing a black robe over your shift.'

'But, Nathan, there won't be time to make one by tomorrow night!'

'I suppose not,' Nathan scratched his head. 'Of course, you could always wear Marge's. She certainly won't be needing it.'

Sophie shivered as she remembered the slashed and bloodstained robe, which she'd last seen lying on the stage.

They stayed at the hospital until they were certain Marge was out of danger. Before they left, Marge, her side securely bandaged, a drip installed to replace her lost blood, and having been given a painkiller, was safely asleep in her hospital bed.

It was almost two o'clock when Nathan's car finally nosed its way out of the hospital car-park. They had hardly been on the road more than a few minutes before Sophie, mesmerized by the rhythmic movement of the car's windscreen wipers as they fought a losing battle against the torrential downpour, nodded off to sleep. Not even the noise from showers of spray, which the car sent up as it hit puddle after puddle, could wake her.

Nathan didn't nudge her awake until he turned into Sophie's road. Sleepily, she thanked him, wished him good night and, flinching against the cold, stinging rain, tottered up the steep steps to her front door. She was about to close it, when a movement across the road, just inside the park railings, caught her eye. Although it was difficult, peering through the darkness and the driving rain, to see properly, Sophie could have sworn the figure she'd spotted lurking behind a tree trunk was far too tall for Carl. It could only be Oliver.

Having made sure the front door was securely locked, Sophie hurried upstairs and, without putting on her own lights, she crossed over to the drenched window panes and cautiously looked out. But by then there was no sign of him. Before she put on the lights, Sophie closed her curtains, deeply regretting that the park had become such a threatening place. Though she was exhausted, after she had dried her hair, got into bed and switched the lights off, she lay awake for some time, mulling over the night's events.

Sophie was suddenly brought out of a dozing, uneasy sleep by a noise outside her window. Was it just the sash-window being rattled by the wind and rain? Or had someone climbed up the trellis and on to the little balcony outside the window? Hardly daring to breathe, Sophie listened hard. There it was again. A scraping sound, accompanied by a several soft thumps, as if someone was trying to quietly drive something into the gap between the frame and the window in order to prise it open.

Determined to find out once and for all who was persecuting her, Sophie leapt out of bed and raced towards the window. But in her haste and in the dark, she caught her foot in the flex of the bedside light and tripped, bringing it, and herself, crashing noisily to the floor.

By the time she had recovered, scrambled over to the window and flung open the curtains, whoever had been on the balcony must have jumped off, down into the garden, and fled. The rain-soaked street was deserted and the only movement she could see in the park was of the wind-tossed trees and bushes. Sophie switched on the main lights, checked the burglar-proof locks were still in position on the windows, and wearily closed the curtains.

In spite of all her past resolutions about not running away again, Sophie decided she had had enough. If she kept living her life like this, under constant threat, never knowing who she could trust, she knew it would eventually drive her mad. She no longer cared whether it was Carl or Oliver who was trying to kill her.

On Sunday she'd pack her bags in readiness and the moment the last performance ended she would quietly leave town. That way she would be free of both of them.

Twelve

Dawn had barely broken when Sophie sat bolt upright.
Somebody was outside the window again. She'd spent
what little was left of the night, sleeping with the
lights on, huddled under the duvet, in her armchair.

Hastily, she flung back the curtains, only to find,
yet again, that the balcony, lit by a pale, watery
sunshine, was deserted. Thinking she must already
have taken the first steps down the slippery descent
into madness, Sophie fell miserably back into her
chair.

Seconds later, she heard another ferocious tapping
on the window, but this time, when she glanced up,
she looked straight into the huge dark eyes of a
massive blackbird. Perched on one of the window's
glazing bars, it was busy viciously attacking, with
strikes of its big yellow beak, an imaginary rival — its
own reflection in the glass.

As the blackbird continued to beat out its hostile,
but futile rhythm on the glass, Sophie couldn't help
smiling. She'd got a lot in common with the blackbird. They both continually faced attacks, real and

imaginary, but neither of them could foretell when their enemies would strike next, or how.

For the blackbird, it could possibly all suddenly end with an unexpected pounce by next door's cat; trapped by flesh-tearing, razor-clawed paws, the final death blow would come from a single flash of its fangs.

And for Sophie . . .? Whatever fate was in store for her, as all her routes of escape and bolt-holes were, one by one, being systematically made unsafe, Sophie was dreadfully aware of the net tightening around her and she sensed time was running out. And the threat was made all the more frightening because, like the blackbird, Sophie still didn't know exactly which assailant would deal that final blow.

Already dizzy from lack of sleep and jumpy with nerves about the impending opening-night performance, Sophie's Saturday morning raced past in a whirl. By ten, having run most of the way through pouring rain, leaping over puddles, Sophie was in the theatre, collecting Marge's black robe. If she had to wear it for the final act, Sophie was determined to remove all traces of blood from it first, and on her way to the station to meet her parents, she dropped the robe into a machine at the launderette.

Inevitably her parents' train had arrived early, and when Sophie tore up the approach she found them huddled together in the draughty booking-hall. Her mother was wearing her all-too-familiar martyr's face.

When Sophie offered a genuine apology for not having been there to meet them, her mother smiled thinly and said, 'Oh, you really needn't have bothered to come at all, dear. I'm sure we could have found our own way. It was you who insisted you'd be here, if you remember.'

'Yes, Mummy, I do.' Why was it she only had to get within range of her mother's laser-equipped eyes to be reduced to the mental age of four? She felt like a conspirator as she hugged her father. 'Hello, Dad.'

A thin man of exceptional neatness, with a polished, pale complexion, his eyes briefly glittered into life, while he almost whispered, 'Hello, love. Have you been overdoing things? You look rather pale!'

'I'm fine, Dad, thanks!' Sophie swallowed hard. Having already fouled things up wasn't going to make the next part any easier. 'I'm afraid the start of rehearsal's been changed to midday,' she said, as they headed out into the wind. 'Which means I can't have lunch with you after all.'

'Oh, never mind, dear,' her mother said brightly. 'Of course, if you'd found time to let us know, we could have caught a later train. We only got up at six this morning so that we could spend more time with you, but it doesn't matter.'

'I didn't find out until the end of rehearsal, late last night. If I'd rung, I would have had to wake you up.'

'Not to worry,' Sophie's mother said with a frozen smile. 'We understand, don't we, Daddy? Your friends must come first.'

Sophie spoke through clenched teeth. 'It's the final dress rehearsal, and I can't possibly be late, otherwise everybody will be hanging around waiting for me. But there's time for a coffee when we get to your hotel.'

'That's nice. It's very kind of you, when we haven't seen anything of you for months, to find a few minutes to talk to us.'

Sophie, knowing there was nothing she could say to make things better, exchanged a secret sympathetic look with her father, and lapsed into gloomy silence while her mother launched into a monologue of complaints about the weather, litter, children who rode bicycles on pavements and car drivers who splashed pedestrians.

Glancing anxiously at her watch, Sophie managed to order coffee before her parents registered but, so that Sophie would know who was in control, when it arrived, her mother insisted on going to 'freshen up'.

But Sophie took advantage of her absence to ask her father, 'Have you seen anything of Carl lately?'

'I see him most days.'

Sophie was astonished. 'But Mummy said you hadn't seen him for ages.'

'No,' he agreed, '*she* hasn't, but I have. Matter of fact, Carl's got a job in the packing section at my factory.'

'Does Mummy know?'

'No,' he said, adding quickly, 'and don't you say anything to her! You know how much the mention of his name upsets her.'

'Over the last few weeks,' Sophie asked, 'has Carl been having a lot of time off?'

'No, I'm sure he hasn't. He's only been taken on for six months' trial. It wouldn't do him any good not to turn up, not if he wants to keep the job, and he's not entitled to any holiday while he's still on probation.'

'So there's no way Carl could have spent much time up here?'

Her father shook his head. 'Too far to drive here and back in an evening, which is why we came by

120

train. No, I'd say it was absolutely impossible unless, like us, he came up for a weekend.'

But most of the attacks had occurred during the week, when Carl would certainly have been missed at work and, besides, the discovery of the sleeping-bag suggested somebody who'd been hanging around much longer than the odd weekend.

On her way back to the Mill, Sophie was so busy thinking about the new information, which completely ruled out Carl, that she almost forgot to collect the robe from the launderette.

The girl was quite apologetic. 'We couldn't get all the stain out but, being black, I don't suppose it'll show.'

'Thanks for trying anyway,' Sophie said as she paid. She wasn't looking forward to wearing a garment stained with Marge's blood, but drew some comfort from the fact that it would only be for the last few minutes of the performance.

As Sophie was about to leave, the girl asked, 'Are you in this play then?'

Sophie felt herself colouring slightly. 'Yes, I play Agnes Wishart.'

'Ooh! I'm coming to see it tonight. I'll look out for you!'

For Sophie, the arrival of her parents and the comments of the girl in the launderette suddenly seemed to change the opening night from a remote possibility to a very imminent reality. During the months of rehearsal, the play had been a private thing they were doing amongst themselves. Just like any group of stamp-collectors or bird-watchers, they were people who gathered together to share a mutual interest.

But what the girl had said changed everything, and Sophie realized that that very night the auditorium would be full of strangers, all watching her. That thought released hundreds of butterflies which were frantically trying to escape from her stomach.

Her stomach's reaction was worsened by the other realization that, since Carl had been ruled out, she would be appearing on the stage with her only other remaining suspect — Oliver. But Sophie couldn't help returning to the question she'd asked herself so often recently. Why him? What possible reason could he have?

Able to find no reasonable answer, she took comfort from the fact that now she was keeping away from him, except for their appearances on stage together, it wasn't really likely he could harm her. But then, Marge hadn't known what was going to happen to her, until it did.

At a quarter to twelve, far later than she'd intended, Sophie jogged across the bridge. She was so preoccupied with her own thoughts, she barely noticed that what, on a previous Saturday, had been a twinkling, gurgling stream, had been transformed into a river so swollen, it was threatening to burst its banks. Sophie was only aware that what, that morning, had seemed like a net closing in around her, now felt more like a noose.

Sophie's hands were shaking so badly that Paula had to pin her hair up for her. But Sophie wasn't alone. Pandemonium seemed to have broken out backstage. Everyone was rushing around the corridors, in and out of dressing-rooms, in a total panic, all shouting at once.

'Tim, have you checked the dagger this time?'

'What was it you said Marge used to do during the burning scene?'

'Who's taken my eyeliner?'

Julian, wild-eyed, charged past Sophie, shouting, 'I've lost my magistrate's wig. I had it a minute ago and now it's disappeared!'

Nathan, a rock against the storm, calmly handed Julian the wig. 'You left it in the loo!'

'Oh, sorry.'

'Now, calm down everyone!' Nathan said firmly.

'What about the last scene?' Angie demanded.

'Yes, it's all sorted out and I'll tell you about it when we get there.'

Pete scowled. 'More like "if", at this rate!'

By way of answer, Tim called through the Tannoy, 'Five minutes please. Five minutes! Beginners on stage, please.'

But from the moment the final dress rehearsal was due to start, Pete's prediction seemed destined to come true.

Everyone was in their opening positions, when Nathan realized they only had the working-light, because Eddie wasn't in the lighting box. 'Has anyone seen him?'

Shaun said, 'He was up on the roof, still trying to fix it, when I came in.'

Tim raced upstairs and eventually returned with a disgruntled, soaking wet Eddie. 'I can't be everywhere at once. Oh, and by the way, I've found out how that thief got into the building.'

Nobody else seemed very interested, except Sophie. 'How?'

'When I went round the back for me ladder, I found somebody's been lifting the old coal-hole cover. I'd forgotten it was there, but all the dirt's been scraped out round it. A thin person could easily get down there and then come in through the cellar.'

'Never mind that now, Eddie,' Nathan said impatiently. 'We've got to get on!'

Eddie wandered up the aisle towards the box, grumbling, 'Aye, well, it's not your tools that keep disappearing, is it?'

Even when they had got the rehearsal under way, all sorts of little things kept holding them up. A prop went missing, Sophie's costume change took longer than before, and some of the cladding came adrift from the front of a rostrum. Next a bulb in one of the main spotlights blew and had to be replaced. All small things, but all time-consuming and not calculated to improve already strained nerves.

During the course of the afternoon, stupid arguments began to break out backstage over the most trivial incidents. First Angie accused Celia of using her special coffee mug. Then Julian almost came to blows with Shaun, all because Julian swore Shaun said a line the wrong way round. People who were prompted insisted they hadn't dried. Others, who *had* forgotten their lines, failed to hear the prompter.

Even Sophie, who had almost no lines to forget, kept ending up in the wrong position. Finally, at the end of the torture scene, she was so busy watching Oliver, she forgot to leave him alone on stage for his soliloquy.

'Sophie! Wake up!' Nathan shouted from the darkness of the stalls.

Sophie jumped, and when she found Oliver looking at her in a rather pitying fashion, she burst into tears and fled.

'Come on, Sophie,' Paula said, trying to comfort her, 'it's only nerves. We're all in the same boat. You know what they say: "It'll be all right on the night!"'

'But will it?' Angie snorted.

With all the catastrophes and delays, it was half past five by the time they'd finished what they could and Nathan had given them their notes.

'But we still haven't rehearsed the ending!' Angie muttered.

'We're going to do that now,' Nathan said.

'Well, I'm not,' Eddie announced. 'I'm off for me tea!'

Nathan tried to physically restrain Eddie. 'There are lighting cues involved.'

Eddie, shaking Nathan off, said, 'You can tell me about them when I get back.'

'When will that be?'

'Seven.'

'But it's curtain up at half-past!'

'Exactly. You'll have half an hour then, won't you?'

As the door closed behind him, Nathan, with a firmly clenched jaw, said, 'Right! Let's get on! Pete, here's your script.'

Pete glanced briefly at the sheet Nathan had typed out for him and wailed, 'I can't learn all that in two hours!'

'You won't have to,' Nathan said patiently. 'You can have it hidden in a big book.'

It was Tim's turn to be alarmed. 'What book? Nobody said anything to me about needing a book.'

'Oh, sorry,' Nathan apologized. 'Any old-looking, leather-bound book will do.'

'But the only one we've got is the ledger the Magistrate uses.'

'Something like one of those old, brass-bound family Bibles would be ideal.'

'They're Victorian, not seventeenth century!' Tim said with disgust.

'Oh, well, I'm sure you'll manage something.'

Tim went off mumbling to himself, 'I don't know where from, at five thirty on a Saturday, when all the shops have shut! Apart from which, I'm supposed to be finishing the lanterns you asked for. Also at the last minute.'

But Nathan, oblivious to the upsets he was causing, started to explain the moves he'd worked out for everyone. The trouble was, they were very complicated. Because Nathan had choreographed them in his head overnight, at home, when they came to try them he'd underestimated the distances they had to travel, and the timing was all wrong. Not only did Pete frequently end up on stage alone, but the noise of pounding of feet, as people hared round the corridors to get to their next entrance, was like thunder.

Though Nathan made numerous adjustments and they tried it several times, it still wasn't working. At one point, when Sophie was supposed to enter with Celia, she found herself coming on with Angie.

'It's not very easy chasing around with these masks on,' Celia complained. 'I keep bumping into people.'

Angie said in a stage whisper, 'But at least they mean Nathan will never know who comes on with who!'

Several people giggled and Nathan swore. 'Let's try it once more.'

But they tried it three more times and still it wasn't working the way Nathan wanted it. Having given Pete a short pause in his speech and Celia an earlier entrance, he was just about to run the scene again, when Eddie returned. 'I suppose you realize it's seven o'clock.'

'We've nearly finished.'

'I should hope so,' Eddie grumbled. 'They're queuing up at the front door already.'

'Then they'll just have to wait!' Nathan said, as he desperately tried to get going again.

'Not if you want an audience tonight, they can't! It's bucketing down out there and I reckon if we don't let them in out of the wet they'll all clear off home!'

'Oh, well,' Nathan sighed, 'we'd better leave it and reset the props for the opening . . .'

'Tim's not back yet,' Oliver pointed out.

'That's all right,' Nathan replied, 'I know where everything goes. I'll do it.'

'But I haven't read through to the end of my speech,' Pete protested.

'I'll come round to the dressing-room and do that with you in a minute,' Nathan said.

'Anyway,' Angie said, in her usual knowing way, 'it's supposed to bring bad luck, to say the last line of a play at a dress rehearsal.'

'Oh, well,' Pete grumbled sarcastically, 'we don't want any of that, do we?'

As they all filed off the stage and Nathan began to reset, Oliver said to Sophie, 'Cheer up! It'll all be over soon!'

Sophie froze. 'What do you mean?'

'The play — it'll soon be over. What on earth do you think I meant?'

'Nothing.'

But as she made her way into the dressing-room, Sophie couldn't help wondering if Oliver's seemingly casual words didn't carry a much darker meaning. They could easily have been intended as a veiled threat. While she took off the black robe and changed into her blue dress for the opening scene, Sophie became aware of a dreadful sense of foreboding descending over her, like a cloud of noxious gas.

Thirteen

The actors had hardly returned to their dressing-rooms before the whole theatre was filled with a lively buzz of noisy conversation as the auditorium quickly filled up.

Sophie sounded shocked as she whispered to Paula, 'There are people out there!'

'That always was the general idea!' Paula said calmly, and then, leaping up, she said, 'Excuse me!' and abruptly left the dressing-room. Moments later she returned, muttering, 'False alarm!' and carried on fixing her make-up. But seconds later she was on her feet again.

'What's up with you?' Sophie asked. 'You're up and down like a yo-yo!'

'I can't help it,' Paula said, as she headed for the door, 'I keep thinking I need to go to the loo! A bad attack of nerves always affects me this way.'

The noisier the audience grew, the quieter it got backstage. In complete contrast to the preparation for the dress rehearsal, when everyone had been running around in a panic, shouting at each other, hardly anybody spoke, and if they did, they were rarely answered. Some stared blankly into space. Others, eyes shut, clutched closed copies of the script, while silently mouthing their words. Those who couldn't sit still, fiddled unnecessarily with already perfect make-up. The remainder wore a fierce look of concentration.

When Nathan popped his head round the door of their dressing-room, Sophie was fiddling, Paula mouthing, and Angie was lying prostrate across the floor, performing her breathing and relaxation exercises.

'I'm just on my way out front,' Nathan said, frantically polishing his glasses, 'Now don't forget – enjoy it!'

Paula gave him a withering look. 'Is that what you normally say to a condemned prisoner?'

'I know how you feel,' he said sympathetically, 'but it won't be like that. The people out there have come expecting to enjoy themselves, and if you do, so will they!'

Tim's Tannoy voice made them all jump. 'Five minutes, please! Five minutes, everybody. Beginners in position, please!'

'I think I'm going to have to pay just one more visit to the loo!' Paula said, as she leapt over Angie's prostrate body.

'Only the sixth time in half an hour!' Sophie laughed, but she knew exactly what Paula was experiencing.

Her own stomach felt uncomfortably like a cold, hollow cave, and yet she could neither eat nor drink for the tight knot in her chest, where the ribs met. Her problem was that she couldn't decide whether her discomfort sprang from just plain nerves, or if it had really been caused by Oliver's remark, 'It'll all be over soon.'

Angie hauled herself up and touched Arnold, her rabbit mascot, for luck. After a final check in the full-length mirror, she paused in the doorway and said to Sophie, 'Well, this is it! Break a leg!'

Sophie was startled, until she remembered that was what actors in American films always said to each other on opening night. 'You too, Angie.'

In spite of all the scorn she'd previously poured on Angie's superstitions, the moment Angie had gone, Sophie reached across and gently rubbed the pink rabbit's threadbare stomach. 'Wish me luck, Arnold!'

But as she walked towards the stage, Sophie couldn't help wishing she had something considerably stronger than a pink rabbit to ward off the evil which threatened her. The way she felt, if the Devil had appeared at Sophie's side, offering a contract on her life in exchange for protection from harm during the next few hours, Sophie knew she would have signed. In fact, as Sophie joined the other actors, all waiting to make their first entrance, she would have given anything for some of the powers the character she was about to play had been accused of having.

The house lights dimmed and a sudden, unnerving hush descended on the audience. The actors in the first scene left Sophie and moved carefully out through the darkness to take up their positions on-stage. Spotlights came up and, from the wings, Sophie heard Pete, his voice a little shaky at first.

NARRATOR: By the time Mathew Hopkins, the witch-hunter, arrived, the town was already agog with anticipation. On a well-remembered, previous visit by

Hopkins, no less than thirty women had been taken into the Town Hall, where they were stripped and had pins thrust into their bodies.

After the awful dress rehearsals and all their fears the play would never be ready in time, it was almost unbelievable that the moment had finally arrived. Whatever was going to happen, the play had actually started.

As the opening scene drew to a close and the moment for Sophie's entrance drew closer, she was aware of her legs getting weak and she was starting to quiver with nerves. An awful thought had suddenly struck her. Out amongst that vast sea of anonymous people, were several she knew. Girls from the office, the one from the launderette, the elderly Mercer sisters and, worst of all, her parents. How could she possibly go out there and then, afterwards, have to face her mother's damningly faint praise? 'Yes, dear, you were very good, considering. But that dress!'

It was hardly surprising that by the time Julian had begun his last speech before her entrance, Sophie knew she was permanently rooted to the spot.

MAGISTRATE: Then I have no alternative. Let Agnes Wishart immediately be brought before this court.

Sophie watched, powerless, as the lights faded on their scene. What would happen when she didn't go on? No Agnes Wishart, no play. But at that exact moment, all the weeks of preparation and rehearsal took over and

Sophie felt herself automatically moving forward. As if being propelled by an unseen force, Sophie stepped out on to the stage and, by the time the lights came up, she had somehow miraculously ceased to be poor, frightened Sophie and had taken on the character of the brave but wronged Agnes. It was a curious sensation, but one Sophie happily resigned herself to. Anything would be better than having to go out and face an audience alone as herself.

Part of Sophie's mind remained. She was vaguely aware of being watched by a sea of out-of-focus faces. But it was also as if part of Sophie became one of them, able to watch herself, and it was undoubtedly Agnes who spoke the first of her few lines.

AGNES: Father, who are these people and why
              have they gathered here?

But from the moment Agnes was brought before Mathew Hopkins, she became totally silent. Something deep inside told her, whatever happened, she must not let this man reach her.

She never took her eyes off Mathew's, and never for one second flinched, even under the most hideous torture his twisted mind could devise. For she knew, no matter what horrors he perpetrated on her body, if she was to have any chance of coming through the ordeal intact, she had to keep her faith with God. That was the only way she could hope to hold on to her soul.

The enthusiastic applause which greeted the end of the first act had barely died away before Nathan appeared amongst the cast in the green-room, where they were hastily sipping coffee. 'You were all fantastic! I'm really proud of you!'

'I messed up my line about the trial,' Celia apologized.

'Nobody noticed!' Nathan insisted. 'Keep it up and we've got a hit on our hands, believe me!'

But all the comments and backslapping washed over Sophie. Her feeling of *being* Agnes didn't fade away with the lights when the act ended, so it seemed perfectly natural to maintain the silence she had adopted. Consequently she found it impossible to mingle cheerfully, in the green-room, with the very people who had wrongfully accused her and hurt her.

Agnes avoided the whole cast during the second interval, and went straight on for the final act.

During her sentencing, she became aware of what, at first, she took to be a rumble of thunder. Only instead of coming in the usual, isolated bursts, this noise was continuous, and the whole stage appeared to be vibrating, in sympathy with it. As she was taken offstage, while the fire was prepared, Agnes was vaguely aware of someone rushing by her.

'Eddie! Who's looking after the lights?' Tim demanded.

'Nathan's doing it,' Eddie said, pulling on a waterproof coat.

'What's going on?'

'Remember my bolt-cutters went missing? Well, somebody's used them to cut the padlock off the sluice-gate's control wheel. They've let the water into the channel, and that noise you can hear, that's the waterwheel turning!' Eddie grunted, as he struggled into a pair of wellingtons. 'Now I've got to try and stop it. But when the river's in flood, once the water's running, it's almost impossible.'

Tim shrugged. 'I think the way the noise rumbles right through the building makes a rather effective climax for the end of the play.'

'That's the drive-shaft you can hear,' Eddie said, 'and it'll be all right, as long as it stays like that. What worries me is, unless I can cut down the amount of water flowing over the wheel, it'll go faster and faster, smash up the governors, and then the whole thing could fly out of control. Even if the bearings on the wheel don't go, the drive-shaft could shatter, and God knows what'll happen then!'

Eddie rushed out into the storm and Tim nudged Sophie. 'That's your cue! You're on!'

> [*Agnes is roughly pushed through the chorus of onlookers, who shout and spit on her as she passes. When she is in the centre of the fire, Agnes is bound to a stake. Mathew, bearing a flaming torch, stands beside her*]

MATHEW: Agnes Wishart, this fire which is about to consume you, is not intended as a punishment. Rather will it force out the Devil who has inhabited your soul, thereby purging and cleansing you, to make you ready and fit to stand before

God. Before applying the torch, I advise you to take this last opportunity to recant the evil you have performed in the Devil's name and throw yourself on our mercy.

AGNES: Having performed no wrong on anyone, I have no need to ask for anything on my own account.
[*The Chorus howls its rage*]

AGNES: I only ask for mercy for those who have wrongly accused me and found me guilty.
[*More howls from the Chorus*]

AGNES: And one thing more ...

CHORUS: [*In a continuous rhythmic chant, low at first, but building*]
Burn! Burn! Burn!

AGNES: [*Shouting over the chants*] I earnestly wish forgiveness for my main tormentor. My hope is that you, Mathew Hopkins, might find the perfect peace I expect, once you have finished with the ashes of this unworthy body of mine.
[*The howls of 'burn' build to a crescendo, drowning out her voice*]

MATHEW: [*Roaring over them*]
Enough! Let the fire do its work and, if you have no repentance on the other side, so be it! Let it consume your soul also!
[*Mathew touches the torch to the faggots beneath Agnes. At first she barely reacts, as fire and smoke rise around her, but then, as the intensity of the heat grows, her body begins to writhe and twist*]

AGNES: [*She screams at Mathew*]
'Tis you who should burn here, Mathew Hopkins, not me. For you are the Devil's henchman!
[*The howls and shouts of the Chorus slowly die down as the lights around the fire fade, leaving the Narrator standing in a single spotlight*]

NARRATOR: But Mathew does not hear Agnes. Even before the flames have done their work, he is busy collecting his fee, and long before the fire is quenched, so that her bones may be taken away, pounded to powder and scattered outside the town boundaries, Mathew Hopkins will have moved on to his next wicked assignment.

In the darkness, the trolley, which concealed in its base

a smoke-machine, a small fan to blow about the fiery yellow and red lengths of silk ribbon, and the flickering spotlights which lit them, was wheeled offstage. But even when Agnes was released from her bonds, she still lay there. 'Come on, Sophie,' Tim said, helping her up and into her black robe.

But though Agnes was dead and the end of the play was in sight, Sophie found it impossible to shake off the dreamlike state of being her. She seemed to be trapped inside Agnes. As she briefly leaned against the wall, struggling to regain control of herself, she was suddenly aware that the vibrations caused by the wheel's machinery had built up, and were not only coming along the floor, but were now also pulsating through the outer walls.

'Sophie, you haven't done your hair, or cleaned off your make-up!' Tim urged. 'Here, let me.' He creamed off her face, dabbed her with a pale powder, and hastily brushed out her hair. 'Come on, you're late!'

Somehow she got confused by the weaving and bobbing of the chorus as they passed Pete. He stood, centre-stage, reading the Epilogue from a huge book, his voice almost drowned by the deep rumble of the machinery. Perhaps because Nathan was still controlling them rather than Eddie, the stage lights were frequently on when they should have been off, and vice versa.

During the confusion, Agnes, at one point, far from floating across like a ghastly apparition, collided heavily on stage with Angie, though only knowing it was Angie hidden beneath the mask and robe because of her diminutive size.

As Sophie ran round the corridor for her final

entrance, she passed a door in the wall which was ajar. She'd never noticed it before, and the cold draught which followed her, suggested the idea that it could be the way up from the coal-cellar. Had it been recently used by somebody? But there was no time to think about that. Celia, holding a lantern, was waiting impatiently for their next entrance together.

When Sophie arrived, for some reason Celia gripped her wrist, but pulled her away from the stage.

Sophie wanted to shout, 'You're going the wrong way!' But Agnes refused to respond.

Celia dragged the meekly obedient Agnes out towards the staircase. It suddenly dawned on Sophie that what was happening was no accident and the person hidden behind the hideous, glowing, skeleton mask couldn't possibly be Celia who, though tall, was thinner and not nearly so strong. It could only be Mathew Hopkins, returned to torment her further. The moment of the final testing had arrived.

Agnes shouted at him, 'Why are you doing this to me?'

Without answering, he began to haul her up the wooden steps. Sophie struggled with her mind, knowing that to have any chance of survival, she had to have control of herself first. But the passive resistance Agnes had set up to withstand her ordeal proved too strong, and Sophie was left, helplessly watching herself being carried away, further and further from any form of rescue. In a last desperate attempt, Sophie managed to scream for help, but her cry was completely drowned by the action of the play and the increasingly loud noise from the machinery.

When Sophie lost her footing, she found herself

being hauled upwards solely by her arm. If it wasn't to be wrenched from the socket, she had no alternative but to follow as best she could. With little protection from the robe and thin shift Agnes was wearing, she bumped painfully up several rough wooden steps before finally managing to struggle back on to her feet. The sound from the stage below them had long since faded. Now there was only the loud, insistent throbbing of the machinery as it crazily whirled and turned throughout the building.

As they climbed higher, that noise was joined by the thunderous drumming of the rain as it hit the tarpaulin Eddie had managed to lash over the most defective parts of the roof.

Shivering as the cold bit through her flimsy clothing and, frankly, terrified, Agnes cried out, 'What harm have I ever done to you?'

But still Mathew held his silence. They had reached the top floor. The noise of the drive-shaft spinning round was almost deafening. He paused briefly before pulling her across the floor.

Any resistance she tried to put up proved useless. Agnes's bare feet simply skidded across the damp floorboards. Where the rain had mixed with the turgid patches of bird-droppings, it had formed a fetid, slushy porridge, which coated her soles and got trapped between her toes. Even when she fell to the floor, Agnes slid easily over it, her robe and shift gathering the foul, stinking stuff up, like a snowplough collecting slush.

Oliver was dragging her past the room from which the rook had come and attacked her before Sophie realized the piercing draught was coming from the double doors. Beside the doors lay Eddie's bolt-cutters. They had obviously not only been used to free the sluice-gate, but also to cut through the padlock and chain which had previously held the double doors shut.

As heavy cloud obscuring the moon briefly cleared, she saw the silhouette of a rope, hanging from the arm of the sack hoist. From the end of the rope swung a noose.

Seth Garner's gibbet was back, and this time Sophie knew she was destined to be its victim.

Fourteen

As the noose hung, ominously awaiting its victim, and the jagged teeth of the crown-wheel whirled round beside them, Sophie had few doubts about the awful fate awaiting her. But she was still unable either to shake Agnes out of her passive response to Mathew Hopkins, or to get back control of her own body, so that she might at least be able to play some part in her own destiny.

The more Sophie tried, the harder Agnes seemed to resist, still blotting out all reaction and feeling. Consequently the battle of wills between Sophie and Agnes was far greater than the feeble struggle between Agnes and Mathew.

But as Sophie saw Mathew reach out and grasp the noose, she changed her method of attack. Instead of thinking about herself, Sophie tried to get into Agnes's mind by concentrating hard on Mr Wishart's reaction to the death of his daughter: how he had said in court, 'Life without my Agnes will not be worth living!' and, although he knew Agnes was innocent, his entreaty to her, when they were left alone in the cell the night before she was sentenced, to confess. 'Agnes, my dear, please tell them what they want to hear, then repent and throw yourself on the court's mercy.'

But Agnes still resisted. It wasn't until Sophie recalled the expression on Mr Wishart's face at the moment Agnes was put to death, that she felt Agnes waver, very slightly.

Taking advantage of that brief moment of uncertainty, Sophie reached up and tried to rip the hideous skeleton mask from Mathew's face. She was convinced, if only she could destroy his anonymity and reduce him to just being Oliver again, then he might not be able to finish the horrible deed he had started.

Realizing what she was trying to do, he knocked away her hand, as easily as if he were swatting off an irritating fly. But in doing that, he lost his balance, and they both fell, until Sophie's back banged painfully against the edge of the open hopper.

The hopper appeared to suggest a new idea to Mathew. Swiftly, he bent down and whipped her feet up in the air, trying to tip her into it. If he succeeded, Sophie knew she would probably slide down its gaping mouth, plummet down the long shaft, and eventually be crushed between the heavy stone millwheels. She could hear them grinding relentlessly away far below her.

To avoid being forced into it, Sophie gripped the sides of the hopper and braced her arms in such a way that it was impossible, no matter how hard he pushed, for Mathew to succeed in feeding her body into it.

Realizing he was unequal to that particular struggle, Mathew released her ankles, grabbed her round the waist and hauled her backwards. The suddenness of his movement took Sophie by surprise, broke her grip of the hopper's sides, and he easily carried her back towards the open double doors. But reaching out for the noose only left him with one free arm. Without hesitation, he picked Sophie up and tucked her under one arm as if she were no heavier than a baby, leaving her uncomfortably looking down at the grubby floor.

As he leant out, the floor suddenly swung out of her sight and she found herself gazing down into the depths of a vast chasm. It was so deep, it took a moment for her to realize the tiny ribbon she could see at the bottom was really the broad river sweeping by. Beside it were a great many people, scurrying around like ants, in the pocket-handkerchief-sized, flood-lit car-park.

But why were they running around in the wind and rain, which was stinging Sophie's face? If the play was over, why didn't they go home? And did that mean she and Oliver were the only two people left in the building?

The wind swung the noose out of reach at his first attempt. He was trying again, when there was a horrible grinding noise from the drive-shaft. Something in the parts below had jammed.

Suddenly the whole building lurched and shuddered, as if it had been struck by a huge demolition ball swung from a crane. Though the shaft juddered back into action, the violent movement of the building threw Oliver and Sophie forwards. Sophie screamed as, with his free hand, he clung frantically to one of the swinging doors, dangerously rocking back and forth over the edge, as he tried to regain his balance.

For several seconds they continued to swing in space, while an assortment of tiles, bricks and mortar dropped past them. Any moment, Sophie thought, she would find herself hurtling through space with the debris, down towards the upturned faces in the car-park. She fully expected him to let her drop, if only to have two hands to save himself, but he didn't.

After what seemed like an eternity, he managed to haul them both back inside and set her feet back on the ground, still gripping her firmly round the waist. At the third attempt, he caught hold of the noose. For some strange reason the method of her death seemed crucial to his plans and, given the choice, he obviously preferred hanging to seeing her simply smashed to pulp in the car-park.

But whatever had jammed the mechanism must have thrown the crown-wheel and probably the whole drive-shaft off-centre. For now, instead of spinning freely, the crown-wheel's teeth occasionally engaged the teeth of the second wheel — the one which operated the sack hoist from which the noose hung. Every time they meshed, a short length of the rope Mathew held was slowly snatched away from him, leaving him holding less and less slack.

Gripping Sophie tightly round the waist, Mathew attempted to slip the noose over her head. Determined he wouldn't succeed, as the coarse wet rope scraped her forehead, Sophie tried to wriggle out of his grip, but he was so strong she only managed to twitch her head from side to side.

Suddenly there was a loud bang, as the trap door beside the hopper flipped open and, to Sophie's absolute astonishment, Oliver's head appeared through the opening. He had scrambled up the iron ladder, still wearing the sombre costume of Mathew Hopkins.

'Oliver!' She'd never been so relieved to see him. But she suddenly realized Oliver couldn't be in two places at once.

Then who was her assailant? Who else hated her this much? Surely it couldn't be anyone else from the cast, any more than it could turn out, after all, to be Carl? 'Oliver, who is this?'

Although Oliver clearly knew, he ignored her. He stared straight at the masked figure, but when he took a step forward, Sophie felt herself being swung out of reach, back towards the open door. Without a word being said, the gesture made it clear that if Oliver dared to take another step, Sophie would be tossed over the edge with or without the noose round her neck.

Oliver froze. 'Take it easy! Let Sophie go. She hasn't done you any harm.'

Sophie was surprised when, for the first time, the hooded figure spoke. 'Agnes is a witch. She cast a spell over you.'

Although it was distorted by the mask, Sophie immediately knew she'd heard the voice somewhere before, but it certainly didn't belong to any of the cast, and she couldn't identify it.

'If we are to survive,' the voice rasped out, 'the witch must be destroyed.'

Oliver shook his head. 'You're confused. That's Sophie. Agnes was just a part she was playing.'

'You're lying! How else could she have taken you away from me?'

'I'm telling you! Sophie isn't a witch.'

146

'If I throw Agnes down into that river,' the voice continued, 'we'll soon know the truth of it. Witches are supposed to float!'

Oliver shook his head. 'Nobody floats if they're dropped from this height.'

'Then let her fly!'

Sophie braced herself and summoned all her remaining strength to avoid being thrown out through the open doors.

But it was the building which saved her. There were several sharp cracking noises from the drive-shaft, the crown-wheel briefly stopped spinning and, before it started turning again, the floor lurched violently. This time it tipped them inwards, sending them both flying backwards, until they banged heavily into the edge of the hopper.

Sophie was lucky. Because she had been gripped from behind, her assailant took the worst of the blow, while Sophie was cushioned. Realizing her captor had had the wind knocked out of him, the moment Sophie felt the grip on her relax slightly, she immediately took advantage of the situation. In one swift move, Sophie ripped off the mask and hood before rolling away through the ooze.

Only when she was out of reach, safely spread-eagled beside the whirring crown-wheel, did she look back.

What Sophie saw by the light of the lantern — green eyes, high cheekbones and black, close-cropped hair — were the very last features she'd expected to expose. 'It's Kate!'

For a second Kate's eyes glittered at Sophie with pure hatred. But as Oliver made a move towards her,

Kate scrambled to her feet and began to run for the open door and the black abyss beyond. Oliver hurled himself after Kate, catching her just above the knees with a rugby tackle which sent her sprawling on the floor.

But just when Sophie thought her ordeal was over, she felt herself being dragged sharply backwards. 'What's happening . . .?' was all Sophie managed to get out before somebody gripped her fiercely round the throat, choking her into silence.

Oliver, who was lying across the violently struggling body of Kate, trying desperately to keep her pinned down, glanced up and shouted, 'Sophie! It's your cloak! It's caught up in the wheel!'

Without thinking, Sophie turned to look at the wheel. To her horror she saw that not only was the cloak caught up in it but, by turning her head, she had brought several strands of her long hair within its grasp. The wheel greedily devoured more of her hair and, in doing so, dragged her head relentlessly closer.

'Sophie!' Oliver screamed. 'Get out of the cloak!'

Sophie tried, but the cord which held it was twisted too tightly round the turning spindle of the wheel for her to free it.

An evil leer of triumph spread across Kate's face. 'Let her to choke to death, and good riddance!'

But Sophie knew, even if she didn't choke, she was about to be scalped. Clumps of hair were already being painfully ripped out by their roots. As her head was pulled remorselessly closer to the wheel, Sophie knew that, soon after her scalp had been reduced to a bloody pulp, the gory teeth would be crunching their way through the cheekbones of her face.

A sudden, violent explosion burst up through the building. The crown-wheel instantly stopped turning and the drive-shaft abruptly snapped off. Several lengths of it were sent hurtling into the air like mini-javelins. They smashed into the roof. Some quivered as they impaled themselves deep in the crossbeams. Others crashed back, bringing down with them tiles and fragments of broken, dusty laths.

More explosions quickly followed as the thick oak beams, which had supported the Mill for over a hundred years, snapped like broken matches.

Sophie felt the floorboards, no longer held secure by the beams, tilt sideways. The lantern fell over and rolled towards her. By its fading light, Sophie watched the outer wall, between the door and window, begin to bulge inwards. Mortar trickled down, like sand running through an egg-timer. Bricks slid out of place and, through the gap they left, a skeleton appeared.

Sophie instantly thought of the mask she'd taken from Kate, but this was no stage prop. Unlike the skeleton masks they'd made, these dry old bones had an orange-brown tinge. The oddest part was, its boney fingers were up level with the grinning skull and looked as if they were helping to force apart the bricks. Almost in slow motion, it toppled out and crashed down across Sophie's body. Sophie let out a long, loud scream of terror, but it was lost in the deep, rumbling roar of the collapsing building.

As the window frame was forced out of shape, its dirty panes of glass exploded in a shower of jagged particles. One roof beam hit Oliver. Another dropped on Sophie, sending a searing pain through her out-stretched leg and she blacked out.

Fifteen

When Sophie came round, she was lying in a hospital bed and Oliver, with a black eye, his face covered in scratches and a bandage round his head, was bending over her.

'You look awful!' she murmured.

He grinned cheerfully. 'Wait until you see yourself.'

Remembering what had been happening before she passed out, Sophie's hand flew up, first to her face, after which she checked that she still had some hair left. Apart from a few scabs on her scalp, she could find nothing seriously wrong, until she tried to move and couldn't.

'You've got two cracked ribs and a broken leg,' Oliver told her.

'People don't stay in hospital just for those.'

'They do when they also pass out and then slide halfway down through a building!'

'How long have I been unconscious?'

'Most of your life,' Oliver suggested helpfully.

'Seriously!'

'Oh, you've only been seriously unconscious for a few hours. It's midnight.'

'Then what are you doing here? It's hardly normal visiting hours.'

'They've just finished patching me up in casualty and they said I could come up for a few minutes, to see how you were.'

Even though he was a little battered and bruised, Oliver still looked rather scrummy, but Sophie wasn't likely to forget he already had a girlfriend. 'Where's Kate?'

'Back in the home, under sedation.'

Sophie was shocked. 'What home?'

Oliver looked guilty. 'Look, Sophie, if you feel up to it, I think I owe you a proper explanation.' Sophie nodded. 'While I was still at art college, Kate and I were involved in a bad car crash . . .'

Was Oliver going to turn out to be a habitual liar? 'You told me you couldn't drive.'

Oliver shook his head. 'I didn't say I couldn't, just that I don't. You see, I was driving the night the crash happened, so I never have since. I got off quite easily, just this scar on my face. But poor Kate was very badly mangled up. It took two hours to cut her free.' Oliver broke off and shook his head as he pictured in his mind the results of his actions. 'Up until the accident, Kate had had a very successful career as a fashion model.'

'She's still very beautiful,' said Sophie, rather wistfully.

'Her face is,' Oliver agreed, 'but in spite of a great deal of plastic surgery her body's very badly scarred. And the worst injury of all was completely invisible. As she began to recover from her physical injuries, we realized she had severe brain damage. She stayed in hospital for ages, but there was very little they could do for her and eventually I found her a place in a private home.'

'Which you pay for?' Sophie asked. It certainly explained the shabby overcoat, which Oliver had thrown over his stage costume.

'Of course I do. Kate's my responsibility. Remember, it was all my fault. I'd insisted she should go to this party, and when we left, I'd been drinking, but I swore I was all right. Obviously I wasn't. I lost control on a bad bend, we ran off the road, and Kate's side of the car smashed into a huge tree trunk. Before the accident, Kate had always been bright and lively, really good fun. But afterwards her character was totally changed and she began to develop these terrible obsessions, particularly about me!'

Sophie sighed. 'She must have been terribly deeply in love with you.'

Oliver looked slightly puzzled. 'In love with me? What on earth do you mean?'

'Weren't you intending to marry her?'

'Marry my sister?'

Sophie's jaw dropped. 'Kate's your sister? But I thought . . . all that stuff about her being obsessed with you.'

Oliver shook his head. 'We'd always been very close, and Kate was terrified that once I'd put her in the home, I'd simply abandon her. Not that I ever would. But she suspected everybody, even the nurses, of keeping me away from her. Then, a couple of months back, she escaped. At first, nobody knew where she'd gone, but I eventually discovered she'd made her way here. She didn't have any money, which was why she broke into the theatre. I still don't know where she got the sleeping-bag from. You see, originally she came to be with me, but when she saw me with you, she decided she had to kill you. She felt it was the only way she wouldn't have a rival for my affections. I tried to persuade her to go back to the home, but every time I got near her she ran away again.'

'I know,' said Sophie. 'That happened the only other time I saw Kate, until tonight. It was last Saturday afternoon; you were arguing together in the High Street, until she ran off.'

'Sophie, I know now, I should have told you about all this earlier, but I wasn't sure how you'd react. You might have, very sensibly, insisted on going to the police, but after what I'd already done to Kate, I didn't want anything else bad to happen to her.'

'I do understand,' Sophie said. 'But I'm glad it's all over now.' She let out the most enormous sigh of relief. 'First of all I thought it was Carl who was after me, and then I thought it must be you who was following me everywhere.'

'Some of the time, it was,' Oliver admitted, gently slipping an arm round Sophie's shoulder. 'Sometimes, when I lost track of Kate, I kept watch on you instead, just to make sure you were safe.'

'Oh, Oliver!' Sophie said. 'And is Kate going to be all right now?'

'Yes. Unless you or Marge bring charges against her. You'd both have every right, after the things she did to you.'

'Oliver, I certainly won't! I'm just so glad it's finished with.' Then Sophie suddenly remembered her last moments in the Mill. 'Where on earth did that horrible skeleton come from?'

Oliver pulled a face. 'Eddie's very upset about that. People immediately said it must be the skeleton of Seth Garner's girlfriend. They weren't quite certain whether the girl was actually dead, or just unconscious, when Eddie's Great-Uncle Seth walled her up in the Mill, but they're absolutely positive now that Seth hanged himself.'

Sophie shuddered as she remembered the noose swinging slowly in the breeze and Kate's attempts to get it round her neck. 'Do you really think the skeleton was once Seth's girlfriend?'

'I don't suppose we'll ever know,' Oliver said, 'but Eddie's even more upset about that than he is about his precious mill.'

'Is the Mill a write-off?'

'I'm afraid so. Kate letting in the water like that, to act as a diversion while she got her hands on you, not only wrecked the wheel, which spun out of its bearings and smashed itself to pieces, but most of the machinery. It was the force of all that happening which brought the Mill down.'

'The thing I don't understand is, where did Kate get hold of the costume she wore? There wasn't a spare.'

'That was Celia's,' Oliver explained. 'Kate must have been watching what happened at the dress rehearsal, realized that it would be a perfect disguise for her, and caught Celia as she was going round the corridor, just ahead of you. It wasn't until we found Celia tied up in the dressing-room, that I realized something was wrong. Even then, until Eddie said the building was dangerous and he got everybody out

154